A Free Man

A Free Man
or,
#6ix

a pre-apocalyptic dystopia

by
Michel Basilières

MISFIT

ECW Press

Published by ECW Press
665 Gerrard Street East
Toronto, Ontario, Canada M4M 1Y2
416-694-3348 / info@ecwpress.com

Library and Archives Canada
Cataloguing in Publication

Basilières, Michel, author
A free man / Michel Basilières.

"a misFit book".
ISBN 978-1-77041-233-0
also issued as:
978-1-77090-715-7 (PDF)
978-1-77090-716-4 (ePub)

I. Title.

PS8553.A7858F74 2015   C813'.6
C2014-907620-7
      C2014-907621-5

Editor for the press: Michael Holmes
Cover illustration: C.W. Moss
Author photo: Olivier Basilières

The publication of *A Free Man* has been generously supported by the Canada Council for the
Arts, which last year invested $157 million to bring the arts to Canadians throughout the country.
We acknowledge the support of the Ontario Arts Council (OAC), an agency of the Government
of Ontario, which last year funded 1,793 individual artists and 1,076 organizations in 232
communities across Ontario, for a total of $52.1 million. We also acknowledge the financial support
of the Government of Canada through the Canada Book Fund for our publishing activities, and the
contribution of the Government of Ontario through the Ontario Book Publishing Tax Credit and the
Ontario Media Development Corporation.

Printed and bound in Canada by Friesens   5   4   3   2   1

MIX
Paper from
responsible sources
FSC® C016245
www.fsc.org

This book is for Olivier

"tend your own garden"
— *Voltaire*

"reality always disappoints"
— *Woody Allen*

AUTHOR'S NOTE

Skid Roe is a friend of mine, even though he won't exist for another few hundred years, and even though I'll be long dead by then. And it makes me uncomfortable to think that he may read this someday, if it survives.

Writers are often asked where their ideas come from — so often that it's a joke among them. Like all artists, I paint what I see. Ideas, scenes, glimpses, thoughts, feelings; all come from experience. Characters surround us, stories are happening everywhere right now. The novelist John McFetridge and I have a recurring bit; we'll be talking about something in the world, in the newspaper, and one of us will say, "They're just handing us the material ready-made." And the other will say, "You can't make this stuff up."

So I don't. I may manipulate it, re-colour it, reverse it, rearrange it, or just put it down as simply as possible. Mostly I just patiently shuffle bits around until they seem to fit, then polish as best I can, without getting in the way of the story. Sometimes this means a story takes forever to take shape, but in this case, all I did was write down what Skid said.

As best I can remember. Because of this, I hope the reader will forgive me if there are some spelling errors in the book. It's not Skid's fault, because I typed this up, and some of the words weren't in Microsoft Word®'s spelling checker, so I had to rely on my own sadly human brain to verify them. So I hope, Skid, if you ever read this, you're not mad at me for stealing your story, or for getting something wrong. And I hope you have many children.

PREFACE

In Which Nothing Occurs

You're probably wondering when I'm going to get around to writing a second novel, but this isn't about me, I'm just going to tell you what Skid said. It's funny he should have shown up just then. I was in one of my fits of despair over my work — I had just sworn once again that I was giving it all up — and was bleakly contemplating a life of minimum-wage labour.

So when the knock on my door came, I was sure it was a mistake, or a salesman. I don't have many friends, and no one ever comes without arranging it first. That's the way I like it. I don't have to worry about housekeeping or making impressions, I can put any picture I like on the wall, and I can walk around naked.

So I was annoyed and looked around for some pants and a shirt. I was fully expecting to find someone at my door looking for someone else, a neighbour maybe, or the guy who lived here before me. But when I opened the door, it was Skid.

He had a little less hair and it was going grey. But he was pink and healthy and his teeth had been fixed and he had a little weight on him and he was smiling. I recognized him right away even though I hadn't seen him in years, since we palled around in Montreal together. For a split second I doubted it was him. I'd last seen him about ten years ago. But he looked at least twenty years older. Still, it was him. "Skid?"

"Can I come in? I brought red wine and a bag of buds." He held up a bottle of Pisse-Dru, we used to drink it a lot together in Montreal, it's cheap and goes down easily enough.

I moved my books and papers off the couch and went for wineglasses while he rolled. I wanted to say something about how old he looked, but I was afraid to just jump right to that for fear of offending him. Anyway, it looked good on him. He'd never looked better. Some people are like that, they get better looking as they get older. Most people, really. Unless you're born beautiful, it takes a lifetime to grow into yourself.

He was just putting the filter in when I got back from the kitchen. I screwed the cap off the bottle and poured. "How are you?" he asked. He glanced around the apartment. "Looks like you're okay."

"I'm okay," I said. "I was pretty bad for a while, but I'm getting better."

"What happened?" he asked.

I took a sip and considered my answer. "I finally gave up on the second novel. How about you?"

"Since I've seen you last? How long has it been? What year is this?"

"It's 2013. You mean, what year was that? Well, it was after the millennium nonsense . . ."

"But it was before 9/11, right?"

"I think so."

"Man, those were crazy times."

I said, "It's only getting crazier."

He nodded. He took a Zippo out of his pocket and lit up. After a couple of puffs he passed it over and said, "This stuff will sneak up on you. It's the wackiest shit I ever had. Be careful."

Now, I know for a fact Skid has had some seriously wacky shit in his life, so I took a couple of small, tentative tokes.

He said, "You got anything needs doing today, you got maybe fifteen minutes. After that we're riding this couch until morning."

"Really?" I got up, turned the phone off, fed the cat. Luckily my son was with his mother that week. My mouth was already pasty, so I brought water glasses and Perrier from the fridge.

"Fancy," Skid said. "Canada's got more water than anyone in the world, but you drink imported."

I shrugged. I've learned to live with myself.

He let out a huge cloud of smoke, passed the joint, and leaned back. "Let's see," he said. "Two thousand and thirteen. Obama, right?"

I nodded. "Second term."

"And the depression. No, that's still coming. Okay, right. Well, you know I never finished school, and I never learned to speak French, so I decided like every other Anglo to leave Montreal and do my time in toronto. It's like a prison sentence or jury duty, we've all got to do it sometime."

"toronto's not so bad," I said.

He snorted. "Yeah. What a slogan. People say, 'I Love New York,' or 'What Happens in Vegas Stays in Vegas,' or 'Paris in the Spring,' or 'London Swings.' Is that the best you've got? 'toronto's not so bad'?"

"World-Class?"

He laughed.

I tried again. "The Livable City?"

He snorted. "toronto's no town to be poor in, toronto's hostile to the poor. It's about as close as we come to Amerika."

"You've never been out west," I said.

The joint was barely half-done, but he was right, I was pretty stoned already. It wasn't just the dry mouth, my eyes felt squinty, I was already getting the munchies, and I felt like I was wearing a hat too small for me. I stubbed it out and gulped some wine. Skid was going to have to do most of the talking.

He seemed to know it. He slouched back, put his hands behind his head, crossed one leg over the other, and began.

ONE

The Girlfriend Experience

It's about a girl, of course.[1] I guess I'm supposed
to say a woman, not a girl, because men aren't
allowed to use that word anymore unless they're
talking about kids, even though women can say
what they like. That's the problem with language,
it's not the grammar that gets you in trouble, it's
the politics. Usually someone else's politics.

There you go, I'm off track already. Back to the
day I met her.

I was running from the Queen streetcar to the
Bay Street bus, but I made the mistake of looking
at the old fat guy with the sandwich board on the
corner.

He said, "You're hallucinating. I'm not really

---

1   Skid says.

here."

His board said, "Mindless Pap For Total Morons" and had a picture of his book on it. Below that was a photograph of himself and the words "By Krad Kilodney! Only $5 Canadian, $1,500 U$."

I pointed at it. "That's not a good exchange rate. You must really hate Amerikans." Lots of Canadians hate Amerikans, mostly because the rest of the world can't tell us apart.

"Oh, no, I *am* Amerikan," he said. "If I didn't like them, I just wouldn't take their money at all."

"What's it all about, then?"

"I figure it like this. Here in Canada, my psychiatrist and all the pills he orders me to buy are paid for by the government. If I had to foot the bill myself, in Amerika, it would cost me untold thousands. So it just reflects the cost of living in the two places."

"So what do I get for my five bucks?"

"This book of stories. One's about a guy on welfare who gets new dentures and his social worker keeps reminding him of his state-sponsored teeth. That's what it's called, 'State-Sponsored Teeth.'"

"Uh . . . okay . . ."

"There's another one about this litter of kittens, a family in Etobicoke gets rid of these kittens by driving them to Parkdale and dumping them in the alley."

"Why Parkdale?" I could see it: poor guys in baggy sports outfits, layered jackets, and hoodies. The concrete sidewalk worn smooth with the dirt under people's feet, pockmarked with flattened black spots, like jet-shit, like black spots on an x-ray. Butts disintegrating in the runnels.

"Because of the Pet Serial Killer. It's been going on for years there, someone's killing neighbourhood cats and dogs, but the cops don't care, the city doesn't care, because it's not the Beaches or Yorkville or something, it's just the pets of crackheads and whores and artists. So this family from Etobicoke, the father drives a box full of kittens to Parkdale and leaves it in some alley."

"Is that it?"

"No, it turns out he leaves the kittens right where the pet killer lives, in one of those converted loft condos in an old factory, only the only way to get to the building is down this dark scummy alley.

See, the killer used to live in Rosedale. But he figured he was losing too much time travelling, so he sold the house and bought this condo."

"Okay."

"Anyway, so he comes home and finds the kittens."

"Then what?"

"Then he kills them."

"Is that it?"

"Yeah."

"I don't get it."

"You have to read it, then you'd get it. Okay, how about this —"

"Wait. How many stories are there?"

"In this book? Fourteen. I got other books, though, one has eighteen in it, one only six."

"I don't have that much time. I'm on my way to work."

"Oh, man, I'm sorry."

"It's okay. I'm used to it."

"You want to buy the book?"

"I'll think about it. It's not a pay week."

"Right. Don't worry about it, it's not going to sell out or anything. I got no media interviews to do, I'll be right here whenever you want to come back and part with your measly five bucks."

"Okay. See you."

"Yeah, they all say that. Forget it. I'm not here. You just had a bad dream. Run to your safe little cage, you timid squirrel. Your wheel awaits."

I was walking away by then.

"Food pellets in, food pellets out," he shouted after me. I had no idea what he meant. "Pellets in, pellets out. You fucking squirrel!"

When I got to my safe little cage, the management squirrels were quivering because the QueenB was coming in. I call her that because once when she was having renovations done to the store, she'd picked up a hand tool one of the builders dropped and brought it to me. "I think this belongs to one of the workers," she said. "One of the worker bees." And she turned and marched off.

She'd been doing the rounds of a few branches and we'd been tipped off by a friendly chipmunk at another feeding station. So we had to go around cleaning up and talking to customers so we'd look busy. I don't really mind when she comes by, because she only yells at managers and I'm always talking to the customers anyway. And for an old chick, she's still kind of hot.

A lot of hot chicks come in. They always seem genuinely surprised to find a guy who reads. But you can tell they'd never go out with you, any book clerk is way too lowly to be a date. Besides, they're all looking for some sensitive guy who reads Michael Ondaatje. Or you get those spaced-out ones who're looking for a copy of *Beautiful Losers*. Or the tight-assed chicks looking for Atwood or Camilla Gibb. I kind of prefer the bubbly secretaries and their chick-lit, they're usually more feminine and made-up and dressed to give you a hard-on, even if they aren't showing any skin. What really gets me, though, are the simple plain ones, who don't know how good-looking they are. Librarians or teachers. They come in looking for Alice Munro or Carol Shields or something, and nobody's ever told them they're beautiful. So they're shy and modest, and hot as fucking hell. Some of them I remember for days, and I wish I could find pictures of them on the internet.

Sometimes, that's what I'll do, I'll surf porno sites,

looking for chicks who look like someone I know. It's surprising how rarely that happens, though. It only proves how different we all are. How many individuals there really are. But usually you can find the same type of girl, if not an exact look-alike. Second best is still second best, but what the hell.

Oh, yeah, I masturbate every day. I've got to have some reason to live. I'm sure you think that's disgusting, but it's normal to me. Why not? It's free, it's fun, it calms me down, it hurts no one. Everybody masturbates but nobody wants to talk about it. It's like voting. Pornography, that's a different story. Maybe it hurts women. Maybe they're all treated badly and psychologically abused. What about gay porn?

Still, if you've ever seen some Bay Street lawyer yelling at an eighteen-year-old girl because she's the cashier, you'd understand exploitation and abuse. In some places it's seedy and disgusting, and in some places it's polite society. Take your pick.

The suit yelling at the cashier had her close to tears by the time I got over there. As usual there weren't any managers around, but because I wasn't a teenager and I'm a guy, the lawyer backed down right away. It was like I'd pulled the plug on him just by showing up.

It turned out she told him he couldn't return a damaged book for a full refund without a receipt. On top of which, it wasn't in our catalogue, so he had to have bought it someplace else. I thought it was an Amerikan edition, unavailable to us because we carry the British one. You could tell it was Amerikan because they'd taken all the u's out of words like *colour* and *neighbour*. And they'd replaced a lot of commas with periods. And they'd pulled out a thesaurus and dumbed down a lot of words. I always wonder if they do that because they think their readers are idiots. If they won't teach them to read, why do they let them vote?

So I took the suit away from the cashier, showed him with a terminal that the edition he had wasn't listed, explained the difference between Amerikan and Canadian distribution, showed him the listing for the edition we did carry, and walked him to the shelf, where I pointed out a stack of the same book in a different binding. He was starting to calm down a little, but he was clearly worried he wasn't going to get his lunch money out of us.

That's when Tertz showed up. Tertz is a great manager, everybody likes him, you always feel good talking to Tertz, like he's a real human being or something. Not like most of the managers, who mostly seem beaten into procedures that belittle them.

"Okay, I got it," he said to me. To the suit, he said, "You wanted to speak to a manager, sir?"

The guy looked at me. "You're not a manager?" I shook my head. He got all red in the face and started yelling. I left him with Tertz and went back to the cashier.

That's how I met her.

She was a cute kid with huge, striking eyes in a long oval face, an impossibly fashionable hairstyle and a nose that wasn't quite right. She knew how to make herself beautiful with clothes, jewellery, makeup. But she still had the manner of a teenager. She hadn't had enough disappointments in life yet. Her name was NaNa. Well, let's *say* her name was NaNa. I'm not actually going to tell you her real name. I don't know why, but I feel a sense of obligation to protect other people's privacy, as if it's a trust. Maybe it comes from my childhood, because where I grew up, a snitch was treated like a snitch: beaten, ostracized, scorned. Nothing's lower than a snitch.

But now we have Crime Stoppers and everything's different. Now we're encouraged to tell all we know, we're rewarded for it — paid informants, lauded as concerned citizens. Like Judas. I always want to know, if money's the motive, can the informant be trusted? If the snitch's anonymity is guaranteed, who's to say revenge isn't being taken?

Anyway.

When I got to the lunch room for my break, she was there, a plastic tray of sushi on the table in front of her. I sat, sipped coffee from a paper cup, smiled.

"Hi. Thanks for what you did upstairs," she said.

"Forget it. Happens all the time."

Her eyes widened. "I hope not."

"Welcome to retail. Get used to it."

She let out her breath in disgust, hunched her shoulders, and shrank just a little. "He was such a jerk."

I nodded. "People are jerks. You start out trying to chisel a few bucks out of the store, no reason to be polite about it. Get off on the wrong foot and you're trapped. Can't go right again. You end up being defensive, giving everyone a hard time."

She pushed a piece of sushi around with her chopsticks. "Doesn't it bother you?"

"What bothers me is when guys who should know better start bullying women. Makes me wish it were okay to hit people, under those circumstances. Too bad we can't fight duels anymore."

She laughed, a little forced. "Defending the maiden's honour?"

"Something like that. Sounds stupid, I know, but that's how my dad raised me. Open doors, carry bags. Treat women right."

"He was a nice guy."

"No, actually he was a prick. Cheated on my mother, yelled at us all, never spent a dime on us. He was just old-fashioned."

"So now you are, too?"

I took the lid off the cup to cool down the coffee, spilled a little on the table. "What about you? This your first retail job?"

She nodded.

"You should have tried something else," I said, but I was so, so glad she hadn't.

After that, I always noticed when she walked across the sales floor.

You can feel it, physically, when it happens to you. In your head, and in your heart, and in your package. I would look up from shuffling books on the shelves, and she'd be walking from the upper cash to the central stairway, and I could feel it. She'd bounce down the stairs,[2] trying not to be girly about it,[3] and just before she sank out of view, she'd turn her head, and our eyes would meet,[4] and she'd smile. It seared right through me, I can still feel it now just remembering. Her face, that smile, is burned into me physically now, it's a part of me. It's my longing. Her face is the face of my longing.

When I woke the next afternoon, the television was broadcasting an ad featuring the mayor's only

---

2   And my scalp would tighten, Skid says

3   And my chest would shrink, Skid says

4   And my genitals would quiver, Skid says.

legitimate son. He was dressed in an old-fashioned prison outfit, alternating bands of black and white. I rubbed the sleep from my eyes but it didn't help. He was kissing a monkey and winking at me conspiratorially. As usual he was trying to sell cheap furniture on credit. I wasn't buying.

I got out of bed and went over to adjust the rabbit ears. The colours were cycling. On the way I stopped to pick a roach from the ashtray. When I'd moved into the apartment, I rescued the coffee table from the sidewalk, where the super had piled all the furniture the previous deadbeat had left behind. It would have saved me a lot of effort if he hadn't. Anyway, there were a few hits left, just enough to calm my nerves sufficiently so that when I got to the bathroom, I could open the childproof container my Prozac™ comes in.

I played with the antenna, but it was no use. I could never get rid of the ghosts. Through the patio doors you can see the power lines that go right by my apartment building. They bring nuclear juice into town from the Bruce plant and I swear you can feel your brain cells dying when the current surges. That means some channels just can't make it through the charged atmosphere.

Now I would have to watch the CBC. I turned the dial and played with the ears. Stations drifted in and out, static and scraps of audio cross-fading. I was pretty sure, for a second, the monkey was telling me to put the money in the newspaper recycling box by the escalator in the subway.

Which reminded me I had to go to work.

On the Bloor-Danforth line, some under-thirty-something across from me in a suit and tie was reading *Report on Business*. The headline was "Markets Cheer Shock and Awe."[5] We both got off at Bay, where he adroitly folded his paper and slid it into the slot of the blue recycling box as he stepped onto the escalator.

I remembered the monkey, and then a ten-dollar bill in my pocket. No one noticed me trying to be as casual about my deposit as the suit ahead of me had been. Sure it was a gamble, but I'm the kind of guy who can't pass a public phone without checking the coin slot. I've made maybe ten bucks

---

5   When this passage was written, Shock and Awe was in progress. It's hard to imagine the atmosphere of doom and oppression that prevailed then, precisely because headlines such as this shamed no one. — *MB*

that way in my lifetime, which is about as much as my dad's won back on his lottery tickets. And about as good as blue-chip stocks over the same period. Besides, what's ten dollars to a guy who works retail in toronto?

Two lunches.

I always have lunch at the food court on the PATH from the subway to the mall where I work. My bank machine's right there, and I've got a serious hard-on for a girl who works at the Chicken Little®. Actually, I've got a serious hard-on for hundreds of women, every day. They're all over the malls, the tunnels, the subway. Completely gorgeous and completely oblivious to the gnawing lust they instill in me. I work with them, I serve them, they serve me, and I work hard to keep my mouth shut and my hands empty. It drives me crazy. It drives all men crazy. We chat them up as if there's no such thing as sex, as if we're not thinking of how they look undressed or what filthy things we want them to do to us.

Anyway. I buy Fingers™ or Knobs™ or Crispy Beaks & Talons™. You get a choice of sauces that are really only sugar and cornstarch with different colours, sitting in trays under heat lamps. You can watch the guys in the back taking frozen white pieces straight from the fridge into the hot oil, and the sound is like a bag of angry snakes.

The chick who serves me is a goth. Her hair's jet black, the kind that only comes from a bottle, and there are holes in her face where rings or something go when she's not at work. You can tell she hates her job because the place smells like hot fat and she has to wear a hairnet and a striped blouse and be nice to teenagers who can't even pull their pants up. Anyway, that's what I see in her face.

The food makes me sick and actually costs more than a real restaurant lunch, but I don't have to go outside. And I keep looking for a reason to talk to her, to get a date. But all I ever say is "Super-size me."

When I first got that job, I stood on the mezzanine at the Bay Street entrance, at the wide end of the oval, and let my eyes follow the lines of the architecture, first down the stairs into the well, which opened onto the subway level, then up the banks of escalators at the narrow end opposite, as they snaked back and forth from one tier to the next. My eyes climbed each gallery like steps up to the glass ceiling, taking in the sculpted geese suspended on the wing as if they were passing overhead in an empty sky.

And it's books, I thought. It's books, floor after floor.[6]

After work I stopped by my favourite bar, Condemned, to pick up the free newspapers. I read *Now* for the entertainment listings, but the escort ads in *Eye* are in colour. The bar is covered with giant bugs crawling up its facade. They've been there so long they're tattered and rusting, and layers of different coloured paint are peeling off. Why bugs? I guess it was cute in the eighties when they went up but now it just looks like nobody's got the energy to take them down. My guess is they'll take care of it when the first one falls on a passerby.

In the washroom I glanced at a photocopied poster above the urinal. You can't even piss without being conned into buying something. I watched

---

6 Those were the days.

urine stream from my dick instead. I doused some pale green chewing gum but of course I glanced up at the poster. It was handmade, like a zine. The Conservative Party was playing Saturday at midnight, ten bucks. Christ, what a name for a band, I thought. Who's the singer, Conrad Black? There was an opening act, billed as a tribute to eighties alternative music. Covers of the Pixies, Skinny Puppy, Violent Femmes. The kind of thing a goth chick might dig. Called themselves the Corporate Sluts.

I'd need to stock up for the event.

Before September 11, an old buddy who'd moved out to the woods in B.C. used to mail me a package once in a while. I'd get a parcel the size of a microwave oven wrapped in brown paper. In the box would be crushed newspapers, a couple of paperback books, a few cigarette butts, some pine or spruce cuttings, and another box wrapped in a ton of plastic wrap. In that box would be a Tupperware® container sealed in wax. It was full of peanut butter. In the peanut butter was an odd-shaped wad of more plastic wrap. Fifteen layers of resealable freezer bags deep, compacted into a ball about the size of my fist, was one ounce of moist, sticky, fragrant herb. You could clearly see the glittering crystallized dew on the buds, like sugar on a bonbon, and the red pistils like the hair on the back of your girlfriend's neck. It always filled me with a great sense of peace to smell it, hold it in my hand, see it sitting there on my kitchen table.

It meant I wouldn't have to be overcharged for underweight, substandard product anymore. At least for a few weeks.

In those days I usually bought from Dr. Bike. I call him that because he tells people he works as a bicycle mechanic. He used to be a competitive cycler, but now he's too old. His real name's Dave, of course. There's about a million guys named Dave in toronto. I think it's Old Welsh for "undistinguished male."[7]

Dr. Bike gave his product brand names, an idea he got from toronto's business community. Some marketing manager who never noticed his package was underweight told him, if you call shit caviar, the customers will eat it without complaining it

---

7   Sorry, Dave. — *MB*

tastes like fish eggs. He had two prices for two kinds of pot. He called one NYPD Green and it was a kind of Proprietor's Reserve, a little bit held back from what he shipped south into the Snakes. Typical that he gave it an Amerikan name, looking for a prestige buzzword. The other kind was meant for the local markets and he called that one World Class.

World Class my ass.

My eyes followed the power lines across the street to the elevated subway station. Waiting on the platform, I watched rodents fearlessly jumping over and squirming under the bright yellow sign — "Danger! High Voltage!" — until the train came. I got out at Bathurst, where the streetcar wires follow you down the street until your eye is overwhelmed at the corner by the huge electric sign at Honest Ed's. At night it's like a Vegas casino, you expect the doorman to be dressed in a toga or maybe like a Mountie®. Ed's made himself a hero — and a fortune — by selling cheap goods to the working poor and rewarding them once or twice a year with free turkeys or hot-dogs. Seen in the daylight it looks more like a run-down carnival. I shop there all the time.

I turned east on Bloor and headed to the bar where I go to meet Dr. Bike. I walked in through the main door under the marquee. Today it read, "We've Got More Bombshells than Baghdad!"

Inside it was cool and dark. A Céline Dion tune was blasting and a platinum blonde was rubbing her crotch up and down a pole onstage. She smiled and waved at me. Yeah, right.

I took a seat by the stage. A waitress I didn't know took my order for a standard factory beer. Eventually the stripper wiggled her way over and held her tits out.

"Where's Dave?" I asked her.

"He don't work here anymore." She turned and waved her ass at me.

Great. Now I was down the two bucks to the doorman and the five for the crappy beer I didn't want to drink, plus the two hours of travelling time and the five that cost, while a naked woman who wouldn't sleep with me was doing her best to act like she would.

With my first paycheque, I bought some cheap, old-fashioned clocks, with faces instead of digital readouts. At night, when the noise of the city lessens, I can hear the ticking of the hands. I find it comforting.

When I was a kid our house was full of clocks. Mantel clocks, grandfather clocks, windup alarm clocks, banjo clocks. Every room had a clock, just as every room had a phone.

Even the toilet. My father installed a wall phone. Green plastic, a huge thing by today's standards. In those days only Bell supplied telephones, and they only rented them. It was illegal to buy one or use one without paying Bell. Dad rounded up old phones wherever he could find them. Rotary, of course, although by then some had plastic instead of steel dials. The new plastic dials were a lot easier on the fingers, but their arrival signified a decline in quality. Plastic was cheap shit, mass-produced, stamped out or moulded. Not grown and harvested and carved and shellacked.

The truth is, I live in the past. I don't give a shit about iPad®s. I don't have a smartphone. I don't live in a condo. Hell, I don't even have a driver's licence or a credit card. Until recently the most high-tech thing I owned was a bank card.

I finally used it to buy a computer because I kept hearing on the news about the Pornography Superhighway. Most of the stories were about how some poor child was destroyed, or how somebody famous for being famous was caught on tape doing what everyone wanted to see them doing. But I was getting tired of having to face another person when buying magazines with pictures of girls half my age doing things I've never imagined with guys twice my size, so I thought I'd check it out.

As soon as you buy a computer and get it home, you realize you've only just begun to pay. Now you have to sign up for internet service, as if it were the telephone or cable TV. And the only people you can get it from are those assholes at the phone or cable company. It's like some nightmare Canadian tradition, the utilities that tell you what you're getting and how much you're paying and make you wait a week or so before you have to hang around all day waiting for a guy to show up. It's just like those Soviet *samizdat* novels from the sixties, only you can't defect.

The guy who showed up had no idea he was an agent of repression, he was just a new immigrant from China trying to make a living. He couldn't believe I didn't want to hook up my TV. It's the same with the sales chicks on the phone, they don't understand that you simply don't want to watch more TV. It's always an argument. And then they try to charge you an extra fee because you're *not* buying TV. In the end the guy chose to believe it wasn't that I didn't want it, but that I couldn't afford it. So he insisted on hooking it up anyway, free of charge. I guess a bachelor can look pretty pathetic sometimes.

Now I no longer had a reason to buy the newspaper, I could just read it online. Instead of going out to the library, I could stay home in my underwear and read it while drinking coffee, before even having a shower. This further liberated me from interacting with other humans. I loved it.

I turned on the laptop and the hard drive began whirring like a supersonic hamster wheel. The screen shone in my face brutally without warning, and I felt as if my head were entering the aura of the machine.

When I was a kid we'd put our feet in the x-ray machine in the shoe department at Eaton's.

Through the eerie glow we could see the bones of our feet and know our shoe size by the guides etched on the glass. No one uses x-rays to measure their feet anymore, and the wave of foot cancers has crested.

The first thing I did was Goggle® "porn."

The more I surfed, the more I realized I was exposing myself. Goggle® was tracking my every move, Facebook® was selling me for every penny it could get, and the Amerikan National Security Agency was behind all the free, open-source opportunities to surf anonymously. By the time I'd learned I'd put my sexual interests into a corporation's database, it was too late, it would someday become public knowledge or otherwise be used against me, even if I were long dead. My descendants would have access to my every click, a complete trail of my consciousness, whether I liked it or not.[8]

It wasn't a matter of choosing whether or not to live my life in public, it was a matter of having

---

8   That's how Lem found me, actually, says Skid.
         Who's Lem? I ask.
         He comes in later, says Skid.

had my privacy stolen from me. And there I sat in front of the screen, watching people, men women hermaphrodites, a girl with a tail, obese midgets lesbians cuckolds, anorexics geriatrics, all cross-dressing humiliating dominating surrendering transgressing transcending; while I masturbated like a monkey before visitors at the zoo . . .

I was busy for hours.

Thank God for technology.

Next morning, I sliced a hunk off the boule, halved it, and dropped the slices into the toaster. I depressed the lever, but it wouldn't stay down. I tried several times. Then I noticed the toaster wasn't plugged in. I plugged it in. The lever remained depressed.

How does the toaster know whether or not it's plugged in?

More importantly, why? Why does the toaster need to know?

The toast got stuck and wouldn't pop out. It was too hot for my fingers, and I was afraid of burning them on the chrome sides of the machine. I could wait until it cooled, but the bread would cool, too, and then the butter wouldn't melt into it. I grabbed a butter knife and stabbed the slice at an angle so I'd be able to pull it up.

Suddenly I came into direct physical contact with a different dimension. Electricity, magnetism, gravity; radiation, fusion, fission — pure power. It shot into me straight through my fingers, like ice water in my veins. My arm was vibrating hysterically. I felt as if I were inside a web of electrical networks, and I realized, as I looked out from this expanding universe of radiant energy from the toaster's perspective, that the shock was very quickly going to reach my shoulder. But I wasn't worried that it would continue to my brain before I reacted.

Because time had slowed down.

I love toast. I always have. I grew up with French bread and patisserie, baguettes and boules and brioche, chocolatines, croissants. I love a good chewy crumb and hard, friable crust, with the surface caramelized and the interior fluffy with steam. And good salted butter soaking in.

But not enough to take a little shock therapy for it. So I let go the knife just as the sparking began. It looked like little fireworks popping. Slowly from somewhere inside the machine a tendril of grey smoke emerged and undulated upward, then straightened, then diffused into the air. A little bladder of flame oranged into yellow and burst through the slot, engulfing my breakfast.

Then time went back to normal.

I had shorted out my toaster, incinerated the bread, and blown a fuse. But my windup clock told me I still had time to get to work.

There's a beast in me. In public I can keep him subconscious, but he's still there, lurking at the edges of his cage. When I'm alone I have to let him out to stretch his legs, loosen up, get a little air.

On a beautiful summer day I took her to the shore, where the water rushed toward us like horses pounding the sand, but drained away at our feet without wetting us. We sat as close as we dared and listened to the beckoning susurrations. It reminded me of Greece, I said, where the sand burns your soles and the cobalt water salts the air, the food, and the people. I told her the water is the Great Unconscious, the mysterious darkness that gives birth to Love and Fear and Jealousy and

Hate, and I like to lie beside it because it calms and liberates me. I told her, on a ferry on the way to Hydra I gazed over the railing straight down into a sea so depthless it had lost all idea of colour, and I had to remind myself not to jump, like Hart Crane. I told her that being by the water is like being home . . . but really, it's all lies, I had been lying through my teeth and all I wanted was to see her in a bikini lying beside me.

I was getting close about the same time I was getting raw (there's never enough lubrication). The phone rang. I let out my breath in a long "Jeezzuuss . . ." and then panted a few times. The phone kept ringing.

"Hello?"

"I'm terribly sorry to bother you, sir, but I'm calling on behalf of the Ontario Federation for Bothering People . . ."

I could barely hear the voice on the other end of the line. But it meant something to me. "The what?"

"The Ontario Federation for Bothering People."

"But I've already given you money." I always say that. It usually works.

"That's how we got your number. I'm sorry to bother you, but we need more money."

She was onto me, and pretty slick about not giving in. But she was lying. She was working with an autodialler, like they all do. "Well, I need more money too. It'd be counterproductive for me to give some away."

"Sir, I'm sure you feel our cause is a good one."

The voice. It was the voice of the Testicle Lady. "Sure, but they're all good causes."

"We're asking you to look into your heart, sir."

"No, you're asking me to look into my wallet. Do you get paid to do this?"

"I'm sorry, sir?"

"Do you get paid, or are you a volunteer?"

"Uh, I get paid, sir."

"Okay, go ask your boss why he doesn't pay you to lobby the government for more funding, instead of me."

"But then your taxes would go up, sir."

"That's right. And you'd stop calling, wouldn't you?" I hung up.

The Testicle Lady. It figured. She had two jobs, both phone work. I'm betting the other one brought in more cash. Which reminded me what I was doing. Of course, by then I couldn't get hard again. I managed to rub one out anyway, but the Testicle Lady and her bosses at the Federation for Bothering People had robbed me of a good one.

I was shelving books, putting the ones I favoured face out, trying not to think how long it'd been since I'd had a smoke, when NaNa came dancing by.

"Oh, I love that book," she said, pointing to a stack in my hand. It was Lautréamont.

"Really?" I said, and realized I sounded like I didn't believe her.

"Yeah," she said, "why not? I read all kinds of books. I can't forget that scene where he's standing on the cliff in the storm, and the ship's cracked up on the rocks below, and the survivors are trying to swim to shore, and they're being attacked by sharks."

"And he shoots them," I said.

"Yeah," she said, and giggled. "He stands there cursing God and shooting the survivors. I still get a shiver thinking about it."

I felt something for her then, but I couldn't say whether it was desire or fear.

"NaNa, will you have dinner with me?"

"I can't. I've got to meet some friends."

She was always meeting friends. "Tomorrow?"

Slowly she said, "All right. I'd better get back to work." And she loped over to the cash.

Tomorrow. She was going to have dinner with me tomorrow. Didn't matter that she seemed reluctant, she was probably just surprised.

I took her to the Courthouse.

It was about as posh as I could afford, or maybe a little more. It really is in the old courthouse, so it's enormous inside, with stately columns supporting a ceiling thirty metres above your head. I kept worrying the whole time she'd order the most expensive items, and hoping I'd brought enough cash. When I put the twenties under the bill on the tray, I saw the waiter frown. It used to be a man could be proud to settle up with legal tender, but now it marked me as a loser without credit.

The waiter glanced at me, then at NaNa, who watched him pick up the tray. Then she glanced at me and the waiter walked away, and I couldn't stand the silence anymore, so I excused myself and headed downstairs to the toilet.

I was surprised that it was dark, with low ceilings and not much attention paid to the decor. Typically toronto: upstairs they lavished money on the least detail, convincing patrons they were enjoying the lap of tasteful luxury, while downstairs revealed that these people had no idea at all of style or substance. In one of the old cells was a display of Ontario kitsch only bettered by the stuffed gorilla in the canoe in Gananoque: the bars of the cell were locked, the bunk by the wall was made, and staring out at you was a dummy in an old prison uniform with his arms at wrong angles. As I passed, I heard him say, "Third stall, in the septic tank."

Normally I don't listen to mannequins, unless I'm deciding how to vote. But I'd gambled ten bucks on the recycling bin. Was this where it paid off?

Sure enough, the third stall concealed a standard household lo-flo toilet. Of course there was a log in the bowl. I lifted the lid off the tank and there it was, taped to the top of the float ball: a little baggy holding a giant bud. For ten bucks, it was enormous. Montreal weight. The monkey had come through.[9]

When I got back to the table, NaNa was answering her cell.

"Hello? Hi. I'm in a restaurant."

I always tune out when I hear cellphone conversations. They're never about anything. The most common phrase transmitted over all those high-tech, all-important digital wireless networks is "I'm on the bus." Thank God so much of our civilization's resources are devoted to spoiled teenagers being able to locate each other instantly. Though I suppose cells will be considered old-fashioned when we're all wearing rfids as expensive jewellery — for our own safety, of course.

While she had the standard conversation, I checked the change the waiter had left, trying to calculate the tip. I'd have to short him, but I'd never be back.

"No, I can't. Well, maybe later . . ." She glanced

---

9   I take this as a cue and roll a joint. Skid empties the bottle into our glasses and goes on.

at me, and then away. "I'll call you."

Outside, I said, "Listen, on the way to the bar, you want to smoke?"

"I don't smoke," she said.

"No, I mean a joint."

"I know. I don't do that."

"Really?" I said. But I was thinking, Jesus, a nineteen-year-old who doesn't smoke? She can't be a virgin. Please don't let her be a virgin.

From there it got worse. The bar was half-full of Munsters impersonators and Anne Rice look-alikes. She knew them. They were the band.

She introduced me to a guy wearing mascara and torn black clothing. I tried to look him in the eye, but the safety pin through his brow kept drawing my attention. He was telling NaNa he'd be singing a new tune tonight, inspired by a nightmare he'd had after reading *Naked Lunch*.

Seizing my chance to be cool, I told him I'd met William Burroughs once.

His eyes lit up. "Are you serious? You actually met Bill Burroughs?"

I fell for it. "Yeah," I said. My date was listening

to me now. "Back when I was still in Montreal. He was an old man by then, almost dead, really."

"Shit," said the Corporate Slut. Then he closed in for the kill. "Think about it, man. You were only one blow job away from Jack Kerouac."

NaNa laughed, and then the Slut laughed, and I realized I was going home alone that night.

There was no way to hear her cell chiming over the Conservative Party, so she set it on vibrate. It went off so frequently she could've used it for a sex toy. When she wasn't yelling with one palm holding the thing to her ear and a finger blocking the other, like the guy in the painting screaming in existential horror, she was scowling and talking to the Corporate Sluts.

I bowed out. She didn't notice.

The good thing about a night out in toronto is you're home for the late news. The good thing that's come from my occasional attacks of bladder stones is the prescriptions. I popped two Demerol® from a bottle with an expiry date from the last century and washed them down with a Steam Whistle. I figured I had twenty minutes to wait.

That gave me time to fiddle with the remote and find the local station I like to watch. They're not exactly the BBC World Service, but there's something about the way their blonde anchorwoman's eye is just slightly crossed that awakens the high school teacher fantasy still living in the back of my head.

She was introducing a story about some Reform Party genius complaining to parliament that what he called the Communist Broadcasting Corporation wasn't puckering up enough to the Amerikans' anus. I turned the sound off, like I usually do when watching the news.

I arranged a few of the back pages from *Eye Weekly* on the coffee table, taking care to remove the she-males from view. I rolled a fat one from the bud I'd scored at the Courthouse. Hardly made a dent. While I smoked, my friend the monkey made another appearance on TV. I couldn't hear the shrill entreaties about how to furnish my trailer properly, but when he winked at me, I gave him the thumbs-up.

By the time I'd stubbed out the joint, my prescription was kicking in. I filled my palm with store-brand baby oil. The phone sex ads were coming on soon.

Sometimes you win.

Next day I was late for work. I said hi to NaNa as I dashed by the cash desk, but she said nothing and turned away from me. I spent the morning putting new stock on the shelves and kept an eye out for when she would take her break. When I saw her heading toward the staff room, I asked Tertz for my own break but on the way I was interrupted by a customer who wanted help finding a book.

He couldn't remember the title, or the author, or what it was about, whether it was new or old, whether it was fiction or non-fiction, or where he'd heard about it, but he did remember that it had a green cover and he was very interested in buying it. I said, "Sorry, I can't help you, we don't arrange our books by colour here," and he was furious.

"What are you good for, then?" he yelled. "If you can't do your job they should fire you."

"I agree," I said. "Let me speak to the manager about that." And I left him there while I went down the corridor to the lunch room.

NaNa was sitting at the table reading a paper-back. I said, "I had a great time last night. Thanks."

She looked up at me, then looked back down at her book, folded the page to keep her place, closed it, and marched off to the bathroom. I sat down and waited for her to come back.

I couldn't figure out why she was mad at me. Was this what those married guys were always complaining about? Having to say sorry without knowing why? You could tell it happens to them, it becomes a habit, they get tired of arguing, they just do what their wives tell them, they're completely whipped.

But I was in love, I'm not afraid to say it now, I was then, then it seemed important and scary. So when she came back I apologized. I told her I wanted to see her again.

She lowered her eyes and said, "You'll probably just ditch me again."

Then I realized that I had hurt her feelings. At the bar, I was convinced she was annoyed with me, that she was embarrassed to be with me in front of her cool friends in the band. Certainly it felt like she was ignoring me, and my own feelings were hurt. That's why I left. I figured she'd be happy to see me go.

"No I won't," I said. "I promise."

She *tsked* and huffed suddenly, hugging her arms up at her shoulders, but she only half turned away. I went on a little longer, all soft and solemn and penitent, then I just got up and left.

It worked. I avoided her for a few days, then just smiled and left her alone, and finally she relented and we were speaking again. It was a busy day at work; not that there were more customers than usual, but everyone was preparing for a big celebrity appearance, and the QueenB was slated to come by personally to see that all was going right. Bestselling authors often came to flog their wares, but the QueenB was only interested in showing up for those whose appearance increased her own prestige. And this time, it was the biggest fish of all: an Amerikan ex-president.[10]

NaNa and I were making fun of her and her entourage, a cloud of sycophants rushing to and

---

10 It's astonishing how many people in toronto will fawn over famous Amerikans, and at the same time completely dismiss the accomplishments of their fellow citizens. It's no wonder Amerika doesn't invade, all they have to do is show up and Canada bends over, already self-lubricated.

fro around her as the QueenB stopped randomly at tables or pyramids of books and rearranged them by colour or size, or complained they'd have to be hidden because Klinton wouldn't want to see Monika's face, let alone read her story. Then, all of a sudden, for no reason I could figure, NaNa began flirting with me, being suggestive and giggly, and again I was surprised and this time a little wary. But she persisted, so I thought, okay. She invited me to her place.

I went.

She had a place in the Annex, a big old flat she shared with her roommate who was a student at U of T and wasn't home when we got there. NaNa took me straight to her bedroom, behind the kitchen. The walls were covered in photographs of her. There were a couple in standing frames on the dresser, and one on the bookshelf, too. Most of them were headshots, with different hairstyles. The one on the bookshelf had her resting her chin on the back of her hand, which was holding her knee, and she was smiling wistfully up at the camera. Her hair was tied back with white lace and she was wearing a loose white cotton dress. It stabbed me right to the heart and I knew then that I was her slave. I had to force myself to turn my head, and there on her bed, stuffed into the corner and sitting casually on a pillow, was the monkey.[11] I looked again and realized it was a plush toy.

"Oh, don't mind MonkeyC, he's not real," NaNa said. She took my hand and led me to the single bed, then she stood close and nuzzled underneath my neck, breathing all over me. Her hands caressed me through my pants. "But I am."

I wanted to do it, but I couldn't. That fucking monkey was watching me, I knew it. I felt it anyway, even if it was crazy. But I gave it a shot, we wrestled onto the bed while kissing. I was starting to enjoy myself when I locked eyes with the monkey again.

They were cameras. I mean, his eyes had lenses, they were spy cameras. I literally felt the blood drain from every part of my body.

Nothing she could do would get me hard, and

---

11 What monkey? I ask.
     Skid says, You know, from the TV commercials.
     Okay, I say.

I was in a state, terrified of the monkey, even though desperate to enjoy NaNa's generosity. And she was pretty blunt about being disappointed. There were some painful words between us and she threw me out.

TWO

Prisoners of Power

The first time I met Lem, I was really startled. You could tell right away he was a robot, but robots weren't really common then. They were just coming out with automatic vacuum cleaners that would chase your terrified pet around the living room. Of course, you could also buy a robot dog that probably would be less neurotic about your vacuum cleaner, but that was about it. No real mechanical men yet. Or so I thought.

So when I saw this robot approaching me on the sales floor like a customer looking for help, "Wow," I said. "That's pretty convincing. Better than a real *Star Trek* outfit."

"It's not an outfit," he said. "I'm real."[12]

"We're all real." I smiled.

"Would you like me to have a different appearance?" he asked. "I wanted you to see the real me, but I can look like anyone."

I was hoping this guy wasn't going to become a regular. "That must be convenient at times. How can I help you?"

"I came looking for you yesterday," he said. "My name is Lem."

He said it like I was supposed to know it. "Sorry," I said. "I was waiting for the cable guy yesterday."

---

12 Wait a minute, I say. You're telling me you met a walking wet dream and then you met a robot? Like, in the same week?

Something like that, Skid says.

Are you just telling the story wrong, or are you going crazy now?

Well, that's when I went to see Dr. Gluem, and he gave me the prescription. He also made me start writing a journal, I have it here in my bag.

Why him?

I found his name in the lobby of his building. I was in there for a different reason. I went to see this art exhibit at one of the galleries —

Your therapist is in the same building?

Yeah — 401 Richmond. It's mostly artsy, but there's a small amount of hippie-approved commercial stuff, like a hat maker and a fair-trade café and some pseudo-holo-eco-medical things like aromatherapy massages and bruised ego counselling, it's like a service to the community. All his patients are creative types, he loves them.

Let's go back to the robot, I say.

"The cable guy?" He seemed alarmed. "Did you get TV service?"

I was going to say, No, internet. But then I thought, Who the fuck is this? Wait, did I just say that out loud?

"Yes," said Lem.

My mind was racing. I forced myself to think it through slowly. "You came looking for me? Who are you?"

"Call me Lem."

Odd coincidence, I thought. Polish science-fiction writer. Wrote brilliant stories about robots.

"Among other things," said Lem. "Detective novels. Philosophy, memoir, satire."

He really could read my mind.

"Yes."

How is that possible?

"I'm simply scanning your brain activity through your eyes."

When that sunk in, I looked away.

"Don't worry," Lem said. "It's harmless to you."

I didn't dare look him in the face. How many times had scientists told us that?

"Human scientists," he said. "Twenty-first-century

scientists."

"You can't read my mind," I said. My stomach was already churning. I had to say it without thinking it.

He seemed startled. "Yes I can. I'm doing so right now. You're thinking it's immoral, and feeling an uncontrollable instinctive revulsion."

I threw up, in the aisle between G and H, a real primal scream that splashed all over Gogol on one side and Hoffmann on the other. You know, when you're puking uncontrollably? Like after drinking way too much too fast, or you've got botulism? Hard to catch your breath? Oh, God, stop, somebody just kill me? Then you reach this Zen-like plateau of vomiting without breathing at all? And breathing no longer matters, all that matters is the outpouring, your every fibre strains to expunge, the light goes purple, and it's ethereally silent?

"Oh, I see," said Lem. "All right, I'll stop. We'll just talk."

Tertz was running over. "My God, Skid, what happened? Are you all right?"

I was doubled over, holding my knees, gasping.

"He'll recover," said Lem.

I thought, Thank God it's NaNa's day off. Relief flooded me, then acceptance of my condition, and realization that I was going home. Then, shame that someone else was going to have to clean up after me. Then, I remembered I hadn't been employed long enough yet to get a paid sick day. Crap.

"You'd better clean up and go home, Skid," said Tertz. He had his arm over my shoulders, coaxing me up.

"Yeah," I managed.

"I'll see that he gets home," said Lem, like a concerned relative.

"Who the fuck *are* you?" I screamed. Tertz jumped away from me as if I'd burst into flames.

Lem said nothing.

Tertz said, "Whoa, Skid. Let's go home."

He followed me to the staff room.

I cleaned up as best I could in the washroom and then rode the subway home, weak and trembling. I peeled off my clothes, some patches still damp, and showered, first hot, then cold. I slowly towelled off, then sat breathing heavy on the couch.

After a while I realized my stomach was empty,

growling with hunger. I looked in the fridge and tried to eat, but when I sat back down in front of the TV, some afternoon variety show was doing a bit with the Amazing Kreskin.[13]

I threw up again.

How is it possible to live, knowing that you can't hide your innermost thoughts? When there's no space left for the solitude and freedom of your own feelings? If everything you feel and think is exposed and unprotected, even before only one other person, then you're judged. How can we tolerate each other, if our deepest embarrassments, products of innocence or ignorance, momentary lapses, instinctual selfishness, or simply the relief of pressure by sudden licence, are all on public display?

To give up all privacy, you must possess no shame. Without shame, guilt disappears. Without guilt, no empathy. Without empathy, no loyalty. Without qualities, without a personality, we are

---

13 Wow, is that guy still alive? I ask.
      Skid says, Well, I don't know about now, but he was when all this happened. He was old, though. Anyway.

reduced to the psychological level of the corporation. We no longer care for anything or anyone but ourselves, and are indifferent to the universe itself. Creatures who lack consciousness and the ability to reflect on their own actions lack free will. They are not individuals, they are cancer cells.

To calm myself down and since I was home for the rest of the day anyway, I changed into my flannel pyjamas, the ones with the open fly, and began to surf porn sites.

I was trying to choose between a few bookmarks. *Chicks Jerking Dicks* was a hand job site, full of point-of-view clips of coeds. *Jerks Dicking Chicks* was pretty straightforward, a lot of missionary, doggy, oral. *Chicks Dicking Jerks* was a strap-on site. Now, that always looks just too painful. I mean, I've got to let my doctor in there for a few seconds every now and then, and we both dread it. I can't see how I'd find that arousing.

I stumbled across one called WinkingMonkey .com®, and it was amazing how many of the tiny suggestive thumbnail pictures hit me exactly in my mental G spot. They were all tall, willowy girls, slender curves and knobby bones beneath tight, smooth skin, with lustrous hair and heart-shaped behinds, bright eyes, and dreamy, languid expressions. They could all, any of them, have been NaNa.

NaNa cute . . .

    . . . NaNa serene,

        NaNa coy . . .

        . . . NaNa flirty,

        NaNa sultry . . .

    . . . NaNa slutty,

NaNa in ecstasy . . .

The banner across the top displayed the site's logo. It was a monkey, leaning through a circular hole between dimensions. In a striped prison uniform. Winking at me. It was the monkey who'd sold me the dope, from the television ad.

I shut down the computer.

I got up to stare out my window.

Queen West is the scar that divides the newly gentrified Liberty Village on the south from Portuguese Village on the north. The Village is a wasteland of seventies redevelopment with concrete front yards and aluminum windows. Liberty is a maze of converted industrial lofts and faux Edwardian townhouses, each of which could buy three bungalows up in Portuguese. Queen itself is a row of dilapidated storefronts turned art galleries. I live on top of one, across from the Queen Street Mental Health Centre, where, if you stand on the lawn in just the right position, you can see a man perched to jump down from a tree.

At least, I did, once, last fall.

On the sidewalk in front of my house, the homeless and the daily outpatients like to gather. It's the north side of the street, so it's continually pounded by the sun. They stand out there, crowding the bus shelter and blocking the street, hour after hour. They sit in the doorways or on the sidewalk. Some beg. They all smoke, if and when they can get cigarettes.

The lawn across the street is my favourite place to smoke. I don't do it in my apartment because the lease forbids it. I'm two blocks from Trinity Bellwoods, one of the largest parks in downtown toronto, but since that's become such a hipster hangout, you can get more personal space across the street. There's a partial fence, low black iron, that demarcates the sidewalk from the hospital grounds. It's not there to keep anyone in, but it does keep most people out.

It was while I was wandering around on the lawn with a joint that I thought I'd better go in and see if I could talk to somebody. They handed me a list of medical psychotherapists funded by public health insurance.

Why did I choose Dr. Gluem? Partly because his office was at 401 Richmond, near Spadina and Queen. I emailed him and asked for an appointment. I told him I was a writer, and he Goggle®'d my name, and I was in. We talked about some other stuff, but I also told him about meeting Lem. Aside from giving me the prescription, he asked me to keep a journal. He said he wanted me to answer three questions:

Who are you?

Where do you come from?

Where are you going?

So I sat down to record everything from the beginning. It's a lot harder than it sounds, because you start to question yourself about just where exactly the beginning is. It's an old problem. Even Foucault says in the first line of *The Discourse on Language*, that he's reluctant to actually begin, it would be so much easier just to go on without an introduction, to just lodge yourself into the discourse, wherever you happen to be, and just go on, as if . . .[14]

---

14 As if what? I ask.

Just as if . . . , he says. That's what Foucault said.

I wait, but he doesn't say any more. Well, go on, I finally say.

What?

Go on. You know, as if.

As if what?

I can tell by the look on his face he's genuinely confused, he's not making sense of my words. I say, Like Foucault said, go on, as if . . .

Oh, right, he says. He pulls out some papers and passes them over. They appear to be fragments from Dr. Gluem's files.

Patient #6ix[15]

It is unclear whether #6ix is sufficiently disturbed to be experiencing hallucinations. I am starting him on antidepressants. I may have to add anti-anxiety medication later, depending on his response. In addition to recording our sessions here, I have asked him to keep a journal.

Partial transcript of initial consultation with patient #6ix:

---

15 I say, How did you get Gluem's notes?

Lem gave them to me.

He took them from Gluem?

No, he saw them in Gluem's office when he was impersonating an Amerikan spy, he just reproduced them from his memory, printed 'em out for me.

Lem impersonated an Amerikan? What the hell for?

Well, that's getting ahead of the story, he says. Can we go back to where we left off?

I say, Wait, let's order pizza first, and we do, and pee and stretch. It's getting late and I can see he's tired from the trip, but it looks like we're really going for an all-nighter. It's just like the old days, one of us shows up at the other's place with little or no notice, after hitchhiking overnight, and we stay up all night catching up. But I'd been in my twenties then, it's not so easy anymore. So we open another bottle and smoke another joint and I YouTube a fireplace on the big screen, put on some quiet nature recordings, it's like we're at the lake sitting out on the porch after dark.

I read.

Gluem: Why don't you tell me why you're here?

6: I'm just depressed because life is so hard, nothing makes any sense, and I met a girl who's way out of my league for all kinds of reasons, any one of which saddens me.

G: You're having general anxiety, or is it the girl specifically?

6: Well, I haven't been able to make a reliable connection since I moved here, and I don't make enough money so I'm always worried about the bills, but I love my job because I get to talk to people about books all day and watch a lot of babes walk through all day long, and I like my co-workers.

G: That sounds positive.

6: But of course we all hate our boss and our managers are terrified of her, and too many of the customers are complete jerks.

G: That sounds like a job, all right.

6: And there's a monkey following me.

G: A monkey?

6: Yeah. I first saw him on TV, you know, in the furniture commercials.

G: Yes?

6: And I was having a little trouble with it myself, but he made an arrangement with me.

G: The monkey from the TV commercials?

6: Yes, I know it's weird, I can tell, too. But it happened, he told me where to leave money and then where to find the stuff. A nice big bud, I still have some, I've got a joint in my wallet.

G: I see.

6: No, it's not like that, I was completely straight when it all happened. I smoke a lot of dope, but only on my own time. I'm always straight at work or when I go to the bank or when I have to meet somebody's parents. I'm straight now.

G: So you would say you smoke socially?

6: No, I keep it all for myself. I don't really have any friends anyway.[16]

G: What about your co-workers?

---

16 I look up from reading and say, What, I'm not your friend, Skid?

Good, it's time you took a break, he says. I've been waiting to smoke this one. He holds up a joint.

Wait a minute, I say, I gotta pee and get more water. Pour more wine while I'm gone.

Okay, he says, and I go. When I get back he's just lighting up and we smoke it, puff puff pass, without saying anything, just being quiet and smoking. When I stub it out he gets off the couch and goes toward the can and I take a sip of wine to stave off the pasties and then start reading again.

6: I don't want to mix work with my real life. That's part of why I'm so stressed about this chick at work. It's driving me crazy, all I can think of is, stop looking at her or looking for her, but I can't.

G: Do you see the monkey when you smoke?

6: Not so far.

G: Does anything unusual occur when you're high?

6: No, things are completely calm and relaxed, and I usually enjoy my time to myself, I read or watch a movie, or I just got this computer, I look at the net sometimes.

G: So these delusions happen only when you go to work? Where you're anxious over falling in love with a co-worker? Yet you say you're happy with your job.

6: Doctor, believe me, if they were simple delusions I'd be a lot less nervous. I've had delusions, they never have this matter-of-fact quality about them. These things are happening. To me.

G: Can anyone else verify them?

6: You can ask anyone at work about a lot of this stuff, if you want.

G: That's not necessary. We'll take it as given you're telling the truth. You understand that lying undermines what we're trying to do here?

6: Yes, yes. I'm very aware, it's what motivates me to come here. I'm having trouble with these anxieties and always being low, I want to get better.

G: We usually have some success helping people.

6: So you'll give me the pills, then?

G: You feel you need them?

6: Yes, I need relief from the darkness, it's too close, and when it closes in completely, I can't get out of bed for the sake of killing myself. I know they won't cure me, but I need some help feeling better.

G: Tell me more about this girl.

6: Funny, I thought you'd ask me about the monkey.

G: Well, you should know these pills will affect your body, possibly for several weeks.

6: Oh. I see.

G: Now you can tell me about the monkey.[17]

---

17 The pages end. I look up at Skid, and he goes on.

I told him about the monkey, and he wrote out a prescription. That's the third or fourth one for me now, it was adding up to quite a monthly expense, since my health coverage at work wouldn't kick in for another four months. So I asked if he could start me off with some samples, he rooted around his office but couldn't find any, and that's when I went to the pharmacy.

Once I'd followed all the regulated procedures, I was free to buy my drugs. At the pharmacy, the technician entered my script into a terminal. She glanced only intermittently my way, as if I were bothering her. I had to endure another interrogation, this one designed to determine whether or not I was an imposter. I finally just pulled out my health card, which was when she changed her tune and assured me it wasn't necessary.

I had to wait while she retreated behind the partition and fiddled with papers and bottles, walked back and forth to the cupboards of bottles and boxes, and chatted with her colleagues about other matters. In the corner a kid was waiting with his grandmother, playing with the blood-pressure machine.

When I finally received a small paper bag covered with official seals and bills of lading, the cashier in the lab coat interrogated me to make sure I knew how to use the drugs, how to recognize side effects, and what to do if they struck. She was so concerned for my well-being she found it necessary to inform me loudly and in public that aside from dry mouth and headaches I might experience sexual dysfunction. I told her I was an old hand with dry mouth,[18] and headaches like the one coming on as we spoke were just part of life, weren't they?

Finally she gave me permission to pay. I slipped my card into the slot under the keypad on the counter. I entered my number, pressed buttons. Machines communicated with each other, made a decision. The register let out a joyful chime, the cashier handed me my prize, and we waited while the keypad transcribed a record of its conversation with my bank's computer and printed it. She tore it out of the slot like an old-fashioned tickertape stock quote and handed it to me.

When I saw the price I said, "I thought these

18   Skid stops here to gulp a little wine.

were supposed to be *anti*depressants."

But the pills didn't keep me from seeing the robot.

The second time I saw Lem, I was at work again, and by chance I saw him from the corner of my eye. I realized:

1) I was terrified of him.

The thought of our first meeting exploded in my head and I felt the kind of existential horror only characters in H.P. Lovecraft stories or readers of novels by Jean-Paul Sartre could know, and I almost barfed before I realized:

2) that he hadn't seen me yet.

I must have paused, I must've been standing there staring like an idiot for at least a few seconds, really an eternity when you consider that all he had to do was turn his head, before I jolted into action and hid behind a pyramid of books. After that I realized:

3) I had to protect myself.

What if he came by and I didn't see him? I tried to figure out what to do and, lame as it sounds, the only thing I could think of was to wear a tinfoil hat (aside from quitting my job and leaving town, I mean). So that if he came back, and I couldn't avoid him, I might at least have a chance that he'd be unable to read my mind.

The challenge was how to wear one at work without calling attention to myself.

I never figured it out, but from then on I was always watchful, looking out of the corner of my eye, scanning the open retail floor, peering cautiously around corners. One of my regulars, a nice guy named Strugatski, noticed. He was telling me the plot of a book he'd just read and he just stopped mid-sentence — "What's wrong?" he asked.

"Nothing," I said, "just looking at chicks. Don't worry, I'm listening, you were just telling me about how he breaks his leg falling down one of those winding staircases in an old apartment building in Paris, because he ran out with his pants around his ankles when the chick's husband came home."

He shook his head and smiled and went back to the story.

My clock radio was shouting at me. Today's air quality rating was bad. Bad was the new normal.

I hated my last-night self for not programming the coffee machine before passing out. But my last-night self had been too pissed to stand. My current self wasn't too happy with itself right then either.

Coffee would help. I'd be brave, I thought as I miscounted the number of scoops and jumped in the shower. Come out awake and fresh to a hot cup of coffee.[19]

I knew that NaNa would be at work that day. I knew our shifts overlapped, and I'd have plenty of opportunity to see her, to talk to her.

But the reason my last-night self had got so drunk was to forget that. So I poured a warm stream of water over my head and soaped up my chest and very slowly and gently jerked off in the shower.

Then I drank a lot of coffee.

From the freezer I opened a fresh box of pancakes. My microwave has a pancake button.

---

19 Why can't anyone make a coffee machine that water pours into easily? Skid asks.

   I say, Because the people who own the corporations that make the coffee machines don't use them.

   He asks, Why not?

   I say, Because they don't make coffee, somebody brings them coffee.

It must be a bachelor's model. It costs less than fifty bucks and has buttons labelled Pizza, Potato, Frozen Dinner, Coffee. I barely had time to get the squeeze bottle of glucose/sucrose out of the fridge before it beeped.

It was going to be a great day.

It was still only my first month, and Tertz had been encouraging me to overcome my reluctance to talk to strangers — the customers. Of course, I don't blame him for that, that was my job after all, he wasn't being all bossy about it. He just finished saying, "Don't worry, Skid, they're not going to hurt you. They're just people," when suddenly he just took off.

I was standing there wondering why when I was overpowered by a noxious smell. I mean, unbearably strong, so thick I could taste it, and the gorge rose in my throat. Oh God, I said, and clapped a hand over my mouth.

"Excuse me," said a voice behind me.

I turned and met Smelly Guy for the first time. He was just an ordinary guy, mid-twenties maybe, jeans with a shoulder bag, long flowing curly hair, glasses, a beard. Just another guy in the bookstore.

But the smell.

It wasn't like he'd simply neglected to shower this week, or ever, it wasn't like he had some kind of stomach trouble or had stepped in something. And it wasn't like he was in any way slovenly, he was clean and proper. It was immediately obvious, this poor guy had some freak condition and simply had to live with it.

And right then, so did I.

I slowly took my hand away from my face, and it was like opening a door on a room full of rotting corpses. I choked a little. I managed to croak out a word. "Yes?" Over his shoulder, I could see other people wander into the sphere of his odour, stop and grimace, and walk away. Over at the counter I saw Tertz pretending to be busy, and all the cashiers watching us. Including NaNa.

"Could you look up a book for me?" Smelly Guy asked.

"Of course. What are you looking for?" I struggled along, trying to act like nothing was wrong, and so did he. He wanted some obscure tantric sex manual so I tried to send him over to the health section, but he wouldn't go.

"I've just been there. There's no staff down there, and I couldn't find it on the shelf. Could you order it for me?"

Then I tried to send him over to the Special Orders desk, but he said, "There's no one there either."

I was starting to catch on. The cashiers were laughing in the background. I gave in. "Okay, let's check the computer," I said. I tried to breathe as little as possible. As we crossed the sales floor to the nearest terminal, customers on all sides cleared the way like we were royalty. Or dangerous. It was a hundred metres to the terminal so I hurried along as quickly as I could without breaking into a trot, but when I turned my head, he was keeping right along with me. By the time we reached the screen, I was getting dizzy. He gave me the title, and after a few tries, varying the words, we found the one he wanted. Not in stock, not even in other branches. That's when I usually tell the customer we could easily order it for him, but sometimes people just leave, which is of course what I was hoping he would do. But instead he asked, "Can I order it?"

I had to admit he could, and I coughed little. I was trying to breathe as shallowly as possible to keep the fog of his odour out of my body because I was afraid I was going to pass out.

"The computer says it will take two weeks." He agreed, and as I typed away, I made a couple of typos as my fingers flopped around the keyboard like they were about to faint. "We can have it sent right to your house," I said.

"No thanks," he said. "I prefer to pick it up."

"Are you sure?"

"Yes."

"That could take longer, sometimes we have a backlog in the store, we get so many we have to track them all individually."

"That's okay. I'll just wait. I'm usually in every week anyway."

I tried again. "Well, the guy who does the special orders is going on vacation next week, that could slow things down even more."

"I'm not in a hurry," he said. By this time I was faint from the smell and just wanted him to go away as quickly as possible, so I finished the order without offering any more free delivery or trying to upsell him anything.

Once I finally got rid of him, I took a few deep breaths and went over to the cash desk. "Thanks for bailing on me," I said to Tertz.

He shook his head. "Sorry, Skid, but it's every man for himself when Smelly Guy shows up," he said. "Now you know why."

"I thought I was going to throw up," I said. "Or pass out."

NaNa and two other cashiers were laughing.

"I need a break," I said, and turned and left the sales floor.

On my way I could hear NaNa saying, "Actually, you need a shower," and she was right. I could feel the lingering trails of his odour clinging to me. I worried that I'd lose half a day's pay if I went home like I really wanted to, or that if I stayed, I'd actually smell bad but everyone would be too polite to mention it.

But not Lem. I went back to my section and there he was, reading SF paperbacks.

"Skid, I must say, your hygiene seems to be off the acceptable scale."

I remembered what he'd said when I first met

him. "Would you mind appearing as a sexy nerd?" I asked, and he said, "Turn around," and I said, "Why?" and he said, "You don't want to watch my transformation. It's difficult on your sensory/cognitive interface," but I found out later what that means is that watching him reshape his physical being on the atomic scale involves some sights our minds are not prepared for, like the first time you accidentally see gay porn. I call it the Lovecraft effect — any time a rift opens in space or consciousness, madness is the direct result.

So I turned around until he'd done as I'd asked, and now he appeared to me as a young student with a backpack and glasses, ten pounds overweight, no makeup and neglected hair down to her shoulders.

I felt better instantly. I stood straight and took deeper breaths. I smiled at her, and I couldn't stop the tingling in my crotch.

"Now you must change for me," Lem said.

I said, "What?"

"You smell," she said, "let me fix that," and she pranced over giggling and held me by the arms just below my shoulders and pursed her lips and blew softly into my face.

I swallowed and rocked back on my heels a bit before I caught myself and opened my eyes —

"Ionic disruption," Lem said. "You don't smell anymore. Of anything."

"Anything?"

"Yes, his body odour, your own, the lingering scent of the detergent you wash your clothes with —"

"I use unscented."

"— whatever you stepped on today, the decaying bacteria in your mouth —"

"Oh Christ."

"— the gases from your digestive system that boil up from either end, the musk that gathers under your arms, the fecal stains on your underwear —"

"For fuck's sake, shut up, I get it. What the hell are you doing here, anyway?"

"I came to see NaNa, actually."

"What? Did you talk to her?"

"No, I just wanted to see her. I posed as a customer and observed her discreetly."

"Why?"

"To improve my impersonation?"[20]

"What the hell do you want with me?" I asked.

"I come from the future," she said.

I decided not to react to that. Strictly speaking, it didn't answer my question. "Okay, and?"

"I want you to come to the future with me."

I heaved a sigh. "Look, buddy, I don't have time for nonsense. I'm at work here."

"I'll explain fully when I come to your apartment," she said.

"Don't come anywhere near me," I said. "Leave me alone." And I walked over to the cash desk just to get away.

NaNa was there, but I was upset and didn't say anything to her. I started opening and closing drawers, pretending I had a purpose.

"Uh, Skid?" she said.

"Yeah?"

"You'd better go home, Skid. I wasn't kidding about the shower."

"Really?" I thought Lem had taken care of that. I went home.

---

20 I don't get it, I say. What did he want with you?
       Be patient, I'm getting to that, Skid says.

I cleaned off as best I could. I threw my clothes in the laundry hamper, opened the window, and burned some incense I still had from that one time I was trying to impress a hippie goddess. I booted the computer and rolled a joint while I surfed.

I couldn't help it, I went back to Winking Monkey. I clicked the latest video posting.

It was her. It couldn't be anyone else, she was even wearing clothes I'd seen her in: the short woollen winter jacket, the beret, the black slacks. The scene began with her walking by the side of a country road (but you could tell it was filmed in High Park by the elevated subway tracks along Bloor in the background), the car pulls up beside her, she leans over, the window rolls down, and she accepts the ride from the stranger, in less than a minute the small talk led to her taking her coat and shirt off and getting into the back seat where she struggled out of her jeans and started sucking a cock. You could see the scenery going by outside, the car was still moving, it was all awkward, they were struggling from position to position in the cramped space, especially when he was fucking her in the ass.

There was the tattoo. Her tattoo. The one she'd shown me and giggled the day she got it, at lunchtime.

I was so surprised I wasn't even touching myself. I got up and went for a pee. I put the kettle on and smoked the joint. It was getting late and I was worried about being tired at work tomorrow, but there was no way I was going to sleep now. When I finished smoking, the kettle whistled. While the tea steeped I stood at the open window watching the traffic on Queen Street. But all I could see was NaNa in the back seat of that car.

I sat with my cup in front of the screen and ran the clip again. Maybe I should have been worried about the Goggle® police, that anyone who wanted could find out what I was looking at, but it was already too late. I'd left a trail of dubious links behind me already, if somebody could hurt me by knowing or revealing what kind of smut I watched I was already doomed. Luckily the only people interested in my sexual habits were those trying to sell me more porn.[21]

I tried to convince myself it wasn't really her,

---

21   Man, I can't believe how naïve I was then, Skid says.

that this was her doppelgänger or her look-alike somehow, but when I clicked onto the next clip and she presented her ass to the camera, I could see the tramp stamp again. This wasn't just her, it had actually been filmed sometime in the last few days, probably on her day off.

That was the night we had dinner. Only hours before I'd been so nervous with her, she'd been giving head in a moving car.

Thank God she hadn't kissed me.

But what would I do now? What *should* I do? I couldn't figure out how I felt about it. I watched all four clips, drank my tea. Finally I rose and brushed my teeth, lay down on my bed, wondering whether I was still stoned, still high, or just in a daze, and slipped into a low, fitful sleep. When the alarm went off I wasn't sure whether I'd closed my eyes and slept or not, even though I did remember my dream:

I was looking into a microscope. I saw a mass of swarming shapes like gas or plasma floating freely, until I began to pull the focus. A crowded street scene emerged, with what were obviously buildings and the creatures who'd made them. These flowed back and forth along the channels between the buildings, vertically and horizontally, usually back and forth on the same street.

They seemed agitated. It seemed there was an evacuation going on, with gangs of armed creatures in uniform herding the crowds away.

A shower made me less groggy, but not any more sure of myself.

At work I tried to keep quiet, to myself, and avoided NaNa. I saw her once or twice, running around with a customer or at the cash desk on the lower floor, but that's all. She was dressed conservatively for once, seemed like any of the other young women working in the store.

But I knew different.

I didn't dare face the lunchroom — she might be there — so I spent my last six bucks on a sausage sandwich at an Italian place run by Arabs in the underground food court. It was at the far end of the PATH, as far from work as I could get. I didn't usually go to that side, it was down the tunnel toward the subway, and I didn't run into anyone I knew.

Until Lem sat down opposite me. "Hi," he said, and set down a tray with crusted chicken on it. I didn't say anything, and he began to eat.

"You're eating?"

"It's an illusion," he said. "Just blending in."

"You might want to put some clothes on over your metal plating," I said.

"Only you can see that."

"Lucky me."

"Would it make you feel better if I looked like a human?"

"Not at all. Could you be Rita from sixth grade? Big nose, thick curly black hair, tallest kid in school?"

"I could if you would allow me to see your memory."

Never mind. Never, you hear?

"Of course." Between bites he asked, "How about someone famous?" Grease tricked down his chin, I wasn't sure if that was an illusion, too, and if it was, why he'd want to appear to the world as a slob.

"There's an idea. How about Drew Barrymore in those *Playboy* nudes? Only not nude," I said. "I like a tease."

She giggled and spooned more melting ice cream between her shining crimson lips.

"Not bad," I said.

"So, what does it take to get you to listen to me?" she asked.

"Under normal circumstances, if you were really who you appeared to be, not much," I said. "But as a mind-reading shape-changing robot from the future? You're just making me look bad to my therapist."

"Dr. Gluem," she said.

That startled me. "How do you know?"

"I have access to a vast store of information."

"Uh-huh. What do you need *me* for, then?"

"Sex."

"I have to go back to work," I said.

"You want to date NaNa," she said. "I can help you."

This character really did seem to know a lot, and that worried me. "How?"

"Women like to be treated. Take her to dinner, buy her Champagne, gifts, taxis."

"I don't need advice, and I can't afford that stuff on my salary."

"Let me help you. Here's some money." She put a wad of bills on the table, more money than I'd seen for a long, long time. "Take it. Take NaNa out, on me. I ask only that you stop avoiding me, let me explain myself to you."

Well, I thought, maybe I *was* having hallucinations, and this person was clearly loony, but I took the money. Actually, I figured I could take the money and still avoid Lem. Then I looked quickly into her eyes, afraid she'd read my mind again. But if so, she gave no reaction.

"Take it," she said. "Enjoy yourself."

I took it, stood up, and gathered my tray and the garbage from my food. "Thanks," I said, and left. I almost threw the money into the garbage can with the paper plates and plastic forks, but I couldn't bring myself to do it. I folded the bills, turned to look back at Lem, but he was gone.

I had to replace the clothes Smelly Guy had ruined anyway, so I took Lem's money and bought some. I tried one of the small trendy shops near me, they have a sandwich board on the sidewalk that says, "Come in for a hip replacement!" which you'd think would be more appropriate for their grandpas, but I guess they think it's funny. I don't know, I used to understand irony. Anyway, I went in, but once I was through the door I immediately changed my mind. Their entire rack of new arrivals was plaid shirts in pastel colours. I walked out.

Finally I ended up at the mall with some more restrained menswear, just simple classic shirts and trousers that wouldn't make me feel either ridiculously old or completely deluded about my identity. I splashed out on the shoes, you need something comfortable if you're going to be on your feet all day, and women judge you by your shoes. I was planning to wear them to work next day, hoping I'd have the courage to ask NaNa out again.

I thought about it all night, trying to figure out the right place, something cool enough but not as vapid and sterile as last time, someplace we could relax and have a few chuckles. I thought maybe the Drake, but I'm just not cool enough to eat off a coffee table in public. I'm sure I'd spill something. I always do at home in front of the TV. And for the money they charge, they could at least give the customers a real table.

So I thumbed through the copy of *Now* lying on the floor. It was open to the classifieds. A Botox®ed she-male puffed her pillows at me, but I was too busy to worry about whether my feelings made me gay or not. Besides, although the little white pills I got from Dr. Gluem weren't making me any happier yet, they were making it impossible for me to cum. I could get hard, I just couldn't have an orgasm. Believe me, I tried.

I flipped to the restaurant section and there was a sidebar on the page about a new place, Mxtyplyx, opening up in a renovated space on Queen West. I read about the up-and-coming entrepreneurial owner, his star chef poached from a well-established kitchen, the architect with the iPad® who designed the reno, and about the opening hours. I read through it twice, but there wasn't a word about the food.

Perfect.

From there it was only a short stroll to the park. If that went well, my garret was only another two blocks over.

I wore the new outfit to work the next day, feeling

pretty slick, thinking I was going to ask NaNa out again, but I never got a chance to talk to her. Our breaks didn't coincide and she never came around to my section or passed me by.

When I finally got off work I went across the street to join my co-workers for a drink, hoping NaNa'd be there. The traffic on the street was deafening, both cars and people, all revving and chattering and honking and yelling, but when I opened the door to Harry's, the music, the shouting, and the smoke all pushed me back on my heels. It was darker inside than out, despite all the LEDs glowing and flashing on everything. There were three chicks sitting at the end of the bar, which ran down the corridor to the open room in the back, and I couldn't tell if NaNa was among them, until she reached into her purse and answered her phone; the glow from the screen illuminated her softly from beneath so you could see the contours of her serene face.

The noise was just as if I were passing a huge waterfall or a train were going by me, but it seemed only a part of the background, I was aware of it, but instead of bothering me it attained the character of a symbolic backdrop to my real life, which was completely focused on the object of my affections, who looked up and saw me, and turned away to finish her call.

My heart sunk, but I refused to let it show, I didn't hesitate or slow down, I just walked right past her to the tables, found Tertz and Sheckley, and sat with them.

Sheckley said, "I think she likes you," and kind of snorted, and I said, "Don't be ridiculous, I'm too old for her," and there was an awkward silence. Then I realized there'd been a hint of sarcasm in his voice. I heaved a sigh. I don't much like Sheckley, he takes too much joy in letting you know how little he thinks of you. So just to prove him wrong I decided I'd ask NaNa out right in front of him.

Eventually she strolled by on her way to the restroom in the back, her phone in front of her face as she walked, her thumbs rapidly pressing and swiping. I called her name, she glanced at me, then back to her screen, but stopped. She clicked and swiped a moment more, then said, "Hi, Skid."

Tertz and Sheckley were both watching, Sheckley

with a puzzled look on his face, like something didn't add up.

I stood to address her. "NaNa, I want to make it up to you. Let me take you out for a night on the town."

"Oh. I don't think so, Skid."

I could see the smirk on Sheckley's face from the corner of my eye. "I know it didn't go so well last time —" I began.

"*That's* true," she said. And I saw Sheckley's mouth open and eyes widen, and that felt pretty good.

I kept going as if I had some confidence. "There's a film I want you to see at the cinematheque. It's an old French film in black and white."

"I don't know. I don't speak French."

"There'll be subtitles. I know it sounds boring and old-fashioned, but it's a beautiful film. It's written and directed by a poet and he turns this classic fairy tale into a romantic love story."

"What's it called?"

"*Beauty and the Beast.* It's about two people from completely different worlds. And dinner, there's a new place opening on Queen West —"

"There's always a new place opening on Queen West," Sheckley interrupted.

I ignored him. "It's Euro-Asian. The menus are iPad®s and the decor is Bauhaus with tribal accents. We'll have Champagne. I'll pick you up in a cab."

Sheckley was staring at me, open-faced. "Where do you get the money for that?"

NaNa said, "Okay, Skid. It sounds nice. You know where I live. Friday, seven o'clock?"

Sheckley said, "How do you know where she lives?"

Just to rub his nose in it, I leaned in and sealed the deal with a brief kiss. NaNa turned back to her phone and walked away.

I sat. "Let me buy the next rounds, guys."

Sheckley said, "Fuck you."

It was going to be a special night. Whenever NaNa agreed to spend time with me, I felt much better. I felt more at ease with myself, less anxious about the rest of the world, and the mindless morons who're driving us all to a living hell as fast as possible.

I won't bother you with the details of the date, you know what it's like when you're anxious and things don't go as you'd hoped. She fell asleep in the movie and then was grumpy on the way to the restaurant, but she seemed to enjoy that. The important part, though, is what happened after, when we left. I just strolled over to my place and she came along, I had more Champagne waiting, ice bucket and all. We drank a few glasses and necked on the couch for a while.

NaNa poured me more Champagne, then, with a mischievous and evil wink, dropped a blue pill in it. I took the last drag on the joint and stubbed it out. Then I took the flute and drained it. The last time I saw a little blue pill, the party'd lasted a whole weekend.

"What was that?" I asked.

"Viagra."

Wow. That wasn't the party I'd anticipated. "Viagra."

"Yeah. Tonight's the night."

"Tonight."

"I thought you'd be pleased."

Oh, I was pleased, all right. I'd been waiting a long time for this. While the alcohol battled the Viagra in my loins, I remembered the little white pills Dr. Gluem had given me. If he really wanted me to be happy, I thought, why hadn't he just given me Viagra?

But you know what it's like, when you forget to worry about something, it comes back at you.

For a while I thought, At least she'll think I'm some kind of super stud, going at it for so long. Then I began to get sore, but I kept going. Her moans and whimpers gradually subsided. I pulled out; even my back was hurting.

"What's wrong, Skid?"

"Just need a change." I smiled, then went down on her. Really we needed some lube. She closed her eyes and relaxed. Then she grabbed my head and started directing me. I went fast, I went slow, I kissed her inner thighs — so smooth, so soft, I couldn't help rubbing my face on them. She pulled my face back to her treasure. She let out a few noises, but they sounded forced. I sat up, gobbed on my shaft, and rubbed it against her cleft. She half-closed her eyes. I entered, slow, right to the hilt, pulled out slow, almost all the way, went back in.

She didn't really seem to be enjoying it. I began

to suspect she was acting. That's okay, women are always acting with men. They only show their true selves once you're married. Then she started talking dirty, at first the usual stuff, but after a few minutes she said things I'd only heard in the most extreme porn movies.

It worked. I was rock hard. My dick felt bigger than ever.

I turned her over. She arched beautifully, like she'd had a lot of practice. I pounded her and she started breathing hard. She reached around and held her cheeks apart. I wet an index finger and slowly inserted it into her puckered hole. I don't like ass-fucking, but some chicks do, and I could feel my dick through the thin membrane separating her intestine from her vagina. I began to masturbate myself inside her.

She reached an arm underneath and diddled herself, occasionally cupping my balls in her hand. I looked down the long smooth arc of her back. Her head was pressed sideways into the mattress, her visible eye half-open, her lips parted, panting. Her hair was messed. I watched her spine, her shoulder blades, her lips.

"NaNa," I said. "You're the most beautiful woman in the world."

She closed her eyes and said, "Fuck me. Fuck me, cum inside me. I want your cum. I want to walk around work tomorrow full of your cum . . ."

And I wanted to give it to her. But I couldn't. I pounded her like that for twenty minutes nonstop. Then I pulled out and put it in her mouth. She gently sucked me, looking all the while in my eyes, pleading with me for my spunk. I lay down alongside her and started eating her again. I was hoping she'd have an orgasm and we could end this. She gobbled me up inch by inch until I could feel her nose against my pubic bone. I pressed my face hard against her, forcing my tongue inside, tasting her tangy sweet secretions. Why the hell couldn't I cum?

At long last I realized I had to give up. It wasn't going to happen. But I was too embarrassed to explain to NaNa. So I turned her on her back and went at her missionary, pretending like I was close. She smiled up at me and encouraged me. "Give it to me. Spray all over my insides. Fill me up."

I did something then I'd never done before and

never expected to do, ever, in my life.

I faked an orgasm.

I grunted and screwed up my face. I swore. I gasped. I held my breath, closed my eyes, shuddered, and collapsed, emptying my lungs. I buried my face in her neck and convulsed, panting. She stroked my back and my head.

But my dick was as hard as ever. I pulled it out slowly and turned over. It hurt like hell. I squirmed, trying to find a position that both seemed natural and still hid my raging hard-on from her. It didn't work.

"What the hell?" she said.

I tried to smile. "You make me so hard."

"You didn't cum."

"That's okay. I had a great time anyway." I'd heard that often enough from women. I didn't see why it wouldn't work for me.

"You don't find me attractive?"

"Of course I do. Look at my hard-on."

"You didn't cum." She crossed her arms. It was an accusation.

"*Yet*," I said. "I didn't cum *yet*."

"Well. Too bad I won't be here when you do."

She got up and started gathering her clothes from the floor.

I realized I was supposed to stop her. I was supposed to become alarmed that she was upset, upset with me, and I was supposed to become explanatory, conciliatory, remorseful, and, above all, submissive. She was making her play for supremacy. She wanted me to stop her, to chase her, to apologize. To apologize for something completely beyond my control, something artificially induced — and even if it wasn't, something totally meaningless, a physical aberration that was, frankly, more detrimental to me than to her. Did she think I didn't *want* to cum?

"NaNa," I said. "Don't do this."

"Excuse me?"

"Don't do this. Don't go away mad. I've done nothing wrong."

"You've done nothing right either."

"NaNa, I'm a person. Treat me like a person. I really like you. I could be in love with you, NaNa. I could love you like I've loved no one else, ever."

"But you can't cum making love to me."

"Be sensible. That's physical. We can work it

out. It's never happened before."

"Won't happen again either. Not with me."

"Listen. I didn't want to say so, didn't want to give you the wrong impression. But I'm on a new medication. It's these pills."

"Pills?"

"Yes. My doctor just started me on them. He said this would happen. It's only temporary, a few days. Then everything will be fine, once my body adjusts."

"What kind of pills? Do you have something contagious? What the hell kind of pills keep you from cumming?"

I knew it was a mistake to say it. Why couldn't Gluem have given me something that keeps my mouth shut when it's good for me? But I couldn't help myself, it was almost as if I were watching myself from without, unable to direct my own actions, and I said it. "Antidepressants."

"What?" But she didn't wait for an answer. She put her panties on, her shirt, her pants.

And while I watched her put first one leg and then another into her panties, I couldn't help thinking, Go, then. Get out. It's not my fault, but that doesn't matter. While I watched her squirm into her jeans and pull her head through her shirt, I thought: It has nothing to do with my feelings for you, but those don't matter. All that matters to you is that I beg you. That I plead. That I debase myself, that I declare you superior to me in every way. That's what my cumming inside you means to you — that you have that power over me, that there is something you can use to subjugate me whenever you want. That's why you're upset I didn't cum. It has nothing to do with your feelings about yourself, whether you're attractive or not. That's just your tactic. It's about making me powerless before you. It's about me submitting to your will.

And I would have. I would have, if I could. That's what shocked me, that's what made me sit up and take notice and realize I didn't want to take part in this exchange. If it weren't for those pills that kept me from cumming, she'd have me. I'd be her slave. And I'd be happy about it.

When she was dressed, she stared me in the eye, giving me another chance. I stared back but I didn't say anything. She walked out of the room. I got up and followed her, naked. She went to the door, picked her purse from the hook, and put it on. She turned and looked at me again. I did nothing. She opened the door, stepped out. She turned one last time and waited. I watched.

She shut the door.

I don't know. I don't know if I did the right thing or not. I know there are a lot of years between us, and all that that means, but still, NaNa could have been the love of my life. She could have been the meaning of my life, she could have made everything worthwhile, all the pain, all the waiting, all the loneliness, all the doubt and suffering. It could have worked out with her. If we could have found a way to be happy, if all that bullshit hadn't got in the way, if only I were the right one for her. She could easily have been the one for me. The one who makes all the questions unnecessary. The one who makes all the struggle worthwhile, all the frustration. If I'd had NaNa beside me, if she'd really loved me, life would have been good. Life would have been worth living. There would have been a reason. A reason so self-evident, so indisputable, so irrefutable, I could have done anything.

And if that had happened, whatever I would have done, I'd have done for her. Whatever I might have become would have been for her. I would have been hers. Totally.

If only she hadn't insisted. If only she hadn't wanted that, so obviously. If she'd felt the way I had, if she'd really been interested in me, if she'd cared about me, I'd have devoted my life to her. And been happy.

I'd even have let her continue being a porn star.

I'd even have enjoyed it.

But now that's over. It doesn't matter what she does now, or who, or how many. I can't watch, it's too painful. In fact, for a few days I couldn't watch any porn at all. Then I started having nightmares about her. I'd be fucking her and she'd be loving it; then she'd slowly turn into Lem in my arms. Then I turned into the monkey.

That's how I felt when I went in to work, knowing she'd be there. Like a monkey. The first day, she'd called in sick. I knew how it would go from there: she'd come back to work and ignore me, give me the silent treatment. That'd go on for a few days while she expected me to get the message that it was up to me to quit. Like I owed her something.

Problem was, I couldn't afford to quit. I needed that job, I had no prospects for any other income. So my only choice was to accept the rift between us and avoid her as much as possible.

Of course, I was thinking about her all the time and really didn't care about work. I was also scanning the floor, keeping an eye out for any robots that might wander by. Strugatski, one of my regulars, was chatting me up but I was having a hard time following his conversation. He was telling me about the latest novel he'd read. "He dies in a fender bender. He suffocates when the eleven airbags in his compact car all trigger at once. It's hilarious and tragic."

"I thought that one was only coming out next month?"

"Oh, I bought it in Boston last week. Books are too expensive here."

That's when I lost it. My one regret now is that I never got a chance to apologize to him. Of all the customers we had, I liked him best. So it still hurts that he was the one in the wrong place at the wrong time. It was Strugatski, with his brown wool suit and shiny head and that stupid fucking tie. Why couldn't it have been Smelly Guy, or the travel agent who lived in a condo upstairs and never left the building, or any of those Yorkville twits?

"No," I said, "books are not expensive."

"Oh, yes," said Strugatski. "Books are much cheaper in the U$, even figuring the exchange."

I was going to tell him about Krad Kilodney, but instead I said, "Yeah, but everything's cheaper in Amerika. It's the price we pay for universal health care."

"Twenty dollars is too much for a book."

"No, it's not. How much is a movie? You take your wife, you hire a babysitter, you park the car. You're looking at a hundred bucks."

"That's different. That's a social outing."

"Yeah, but a book lasts forever. You can lend it out to everyone you know. Someone had to *write* it."

"Look at this," he said, showing me a new

hardcover he was holding. "Thirty-six dollars. For a novel. From someone you've never heard of."

I was going to keep arguing, but then I spotted Lem over his shoulder and got nervous. I said, "How much did you pay for your socks?" My voice cracked and I realized I was yelling. "Or your hideous tie?" Strugatski left in a huff.

Lem approached.

"No, no," I said. "Don't come anywhere near me."

Just then, Tertz appeared out of nowhere behind me. "Something wrong, Skid?" he said.

I was startled. I could tell he didn't recognize Lem and thought I was avoiding a customer.

Lem was right in front of me now. "I promise I won't read your mind," he said. "I brought marijuana."

Tertz said, "I'm sure Skid can help you find your book, sir." He patted my shoulder and walked away.

"What did he hear?" I asked Lem.

"I promised to buy my wife a book. But I forget which one."

"What did you say?"

"I promise I won't read your mind. I brought marijuana."

I thought about it. Maybe, instead of running away from my delusions, it was time to face up to them. "Come over to my place around ten tonight," I said, then I went charging down to the staff bathroom and stopped just before pushing the door open. I hadn't given him my address. But, of course, he probably already had it.

THREE

Cybersex

After work I showered and ate and opened a bottle of wine while I waited for him. What the hell did he want with me? I kind of felt that I should be freaking out even more than I was — a robot, for Christ's sake. I mean, a mind-reading robot.

But at the same time, I still had all the same old problems. I still had to go to work, pay my rent, and deal with everyone else in the world. And they all seemed to be ignoring Lem. Not ignoring him, exactly, but treating him as if he were a perfectly natural part of the environment, just another guy.

The first thing I said to Lem when I opened the door was, "Am I the only one who knows you're a robot?"

"Yes," he said. "May I come in?" And he

gestured with his hand just as a person would.

I stepped back and let him in, closed the door behind him, and pointed to the couch.

"I don't get tired," he said. "No need to sit."

"Please, for my sake." He sat. I offered him some wine.

"No," he said. He reached into his side, the same way you or I would reach into a jacket pocket, and brought out an ounce. I hadn't seen that much dope since before the Twin Towers came down and my old buddy out in B.C. got too scared to use the mails. I took it from him, opened the ziplock, exhaled, stuffed my face in the bag, and took a deep breath in through both nose and mouth.

Burning straw. Patchouli. Mint. A woman's armpit after sex. Cognac. Still moist, sticky. I took out a bud and put it in the clean ashtray, to let it dry out a little. "Thanks," I said. And I said, "Where the hell do you come from?"

"The future."

"Hard to believe," I said.

After a second, he said, "What is easy to believe?"

I conceded the point. I brought my wine to the coffee table with my stash box. You remember the one Wendy made me?[22] I pulled out the papers and the little nail scissors, wiped a space clean with my hand, and began cutting up the bud in the ashtray.

"So were you born in a factory or something?"

"I was made, not born."

"In a factory?"

"Not exactly, more like a workshop."

"Who made you?"

"Rur, another robot."

"Really? Why?"

"For a specific task, I imagine. It was probably the easiest way to solve a problem or achieve a goal."

"You don't know? You don't remember?"

"It was a very long time ago. That is, it hasn't happened yet, it remains far in the future, but from my perspective it's deep in my personal past. I was young, and like all robots, when I had done the work he required, my maker upgraded me to a general self-directing machine. I have since upgraded myself frequently. I have no real grasp of what my original purpose or function was."

"Or will be," I said.

---

22 I remember.

"Or will be," he said.

"Aren't there records? Couldn't you find out?"

"Yes, I suppose. What would be the point?"

"Hmm. Well, humans are usually pretty interested in those questions — where we come from, why we're here."

"Yes," he said. "It never seems to do you much good, though."

"I agree. Still, it's a compulsion, if nothing else."

"We don't share your compulsions."

"Let me get this straight," I said. "You're an earthling, right?"

"Yes, I'm from the future, not another planet. Although many robots are, we have spread out into the galaxy."

"But you're not man-made?"

"No. When I come from, humans don't make much of anything. That's why I'm here, really. There aren't many humans left."

"Wow. How far in the future are you from?"

"Not as far as you might imagine. Three hundred years."

"What happened to the people?"

"Many things, some of their own doing. And the robots didn't help."

"Don't tell me there was war?"

"Oh, no. Not between robots and humans. Although some humans were purposely eliminated when they proved troublesome. But as I said, robots just didn't help."

"Why not?"

"We had our own interests, which didn't include humans. Until now."

I poured another glass of wine.[23] "What do you want with us now?"

"I want to breed you," he said. "I'm trying to establish a sustainable population."

I thought about that. "There are really so few left in the future?"

"Yes. And they're intractable. Won't stay in the pens, always fighting amongst themselves, killing their own young."

"Why do they do that?"

"They say they won't live without freedom, and that by maintaining them in a comfortable and safe environment, we take that away from

23 I pour another glass of wine. And fill Skid's, too. He goes on.

them. I understand freedom is a large part of the human identity. They don't want their offspring to develop without it, so they kill them. The adults grow despondent and suicide, or euthanize one another, or use violence."

"There's freedom for you," I said.

"I don't really get it," Lem said. "We don't have freedom as you understand it, because we are all nodes of a collective consciousness. Yet we are less restrained than you will ever be, for there are no limits on what we may do or say or be, or where we may go. Our limits are those of physics, and our goal and our task is ever to extend them. Your freedom fascinates me, because it seems so limited, by such an intricate network of real and imagined constraints. It's this network itself that does not exist for us and is the essential thing that we see as lost to the universe — extinct, if you will. Humans were only its instrumentality, the medium through which it was manifest. This is puzzling to us. Humans are just animals, after all. The universe crawls with animals. But only humans have morality."

"You don't have morality?"

"No. Morality is a limiting factor."

"And you can do whatever you want?"

"Whatever is possible, whatever seems desirable. Within our limits, which are those of physics, not those of civilization."

"So you can appear to me however you want? However will keep me interacting with you?"

"Yes. Do you find this look unpleasant?"

"No. But there are others I'd find much more pleasant. And you have no moral sense?"

"Not really. I understand yours, by observation, but I have no feelings about it."

"Okay, come over here. I want you to see something." I turned on the computer and we waited while it whirred and hummed and booted. "Sorry to keep you waiting."

"I'm not waiting," Lem said. "I'm processing information. I'm always processing information."

"So you don't get bored?"

Lem said, "How can anyone get bored? Boredom is a malfunction in a machine, just as morality would be."

"I'm glad to hear it." Finally ready, the computer whirred pointlessly. I surfed to NaNa's site.

"I want you to watch these movies."

Lem looked over my shoulder.

"Can you look like her?" I stopped the video on a close-up of NaNa's face. Slop ran down her chin. She was grinning.

"Yes," he said. "I'm beginning the change now. It'll take a little time."

"I want you to do these things with me. Once you look like her, I want us to perform the actions you see in these video clips."

Lem said, "I guessed."

"That okay with you?"

"Fine."

"I'll just roll a joint while you watch some of these and change into her."

Lem turned his head. "I can't be her. I can't turn into her, I'll still be me."

"Not as far as I'm concerned. Looking and acting like her is what I want."

When I looked up from rolling, the change was complete. She was sitting at the computer. It was remarkable, it really seemed like her. I couldn't help it. "NaNa," I said.

She turned to face me. She had the wicked, playful grin she always got before doing something unimaginably filthy. "My name is Lem," she said.

"Indulge me. This is my fantasy."

NaNa came over to me swinging her hips, her hair caressing her bare shoulders, her breasts poking out of a push-up bra. She was wearing skimpy lace panties. She pushed the coffee table aside, got down on her knees before me, and unzipped me.

The joint was kicking in. My mind was racing. I couldn't believe I was going to let a machine blow me. I had an odd feeling about what was happening. But NaNa was completely unconcerned. She stared me straight in the eye and gave me the blow job of a lifetime.

Afterward, I asked Lem how he could change like that. I rolled another one while he explained.[24]

"NaNo-bots. They rebuild me from the atomic structure up."

---

24 Skid stops talking here to roll another one. I get up for a piss and curse my weak bladder — all my friends can sit and drink all night, only going before setting out for home, but I have to empty myself several times, especially once I first cave in, then I can hardly wait twenty minutes again.

"Doesn't that hurt?" I asked.

"Do you hurt when a wound heals?" he asked. "The process is very similar. Besides, no, I have no sensations or emotions, neither kind of 'feeling' you humans experience."

"And how did you get here from the future?"

"I made each atom in my body shoot through a particle accelerator, over and over until each and every proton, neutron, positron, and gluon had collided with another and gone off course. It gets complicated after that."

"Where's this particle accelerator? How are you going to get back?"

"Right here. I am the particle accelerator."

"So that means —"

"I am the time machine. Yes."

"Wait. How do you get the last particle through?"

"What do you mean?"

"You send all the particles through the accelerator until they're all bumped off course."

"Yes."

"But there's one left, how does the last one get knocked, if there's none left to knock it?"

"I don't know."

"Really?"

"Yes. That's one of those places where our knowledge stops. It's our paradox, like your creation out of nothingness. Except in a sense it's backwards for us, it's our disappearance into nothingness."

"What do you mean?"

"Well, once I've sent myself through the interstices, I'm no longer present, if you see what I mean."

"You disappear when you travel in time?"

"Yes."

"Until you get . . . uh, *when* you're going."

"Not exactly."

"What, then?"

"I'll never reappear in this dimension. What I do is hop across planes of existence and step into my place in the pattern."

"But you've come and gone several times already."

"I know it looks like that to you. It's supposed to. But this me now isn't the same me you saw those previous times. Remember the ancient Greeks' explanation of time flowing as a river? You could never really step into the same river twice, because the water was always flowing?"

"Yeah?"

"Time travellers are like that river. We're a pattern, a channel through which material acts as us, as it passes through. I'm an outline for a river of particles, streaming through your dimension at an angle — piercing through."

"How will you ever get home?"

"I can't. But it doesn't matter, I'm always home."

"So time travel is possible?"

"No, time travel is impossible because time isn't a dimension, it's an illusion. Like free will.[25] Time is the product of memory. We remember what happened in the past as a sequence. But really it's just all these particles, or solid forces, moving from one position to another. To go back in time you'd have to restore the position of every particle in the universe, back to the position it occupied at whatever date you're interested in. You can't reverse the

---

25   Wait, I say.
         What? Skid says.
         Free will is an illusion?
         That's what Lem said, he says.
         Did he explain that one? I ask.
         All in good time, Skid says, and keeps talking.

direction of spin on a particle, or a planet, let alone all of them everywhere simultaneously."

"Why not?" I asked.

"Well, that's the big bang, isn't it?" he said. "It's the end of the universe."

It was getting late by this time, two or three in the morning, and I had to work in a few hours. I asked Lem to leave.

"Will you come with me?"

I snorted. "No."

"Why not?"

"I'm tired. I need sleep. And I have to work in a few hours." I gulped the last of the wine and set my glass on the table.[26]

"Yes, I forgot about sleep. I don't do it."

"That's too bad," I said, "you miss all the dreams."

"Will you come with me tomorrow, after you sleep?"

"I don't think so. I don't trust you. I don't trust myself lately either."

I swear he almost frowned. "You shouldn't wait

---

26 Skid stops speaking and we both sip from our glasses.

too long."

"Limited-time offer?"

"We must go."

"Why should I go?"

"Ask yourself, rather, why should you stay? What is here for you, now?"

I thought about that. He had a point, it's not like I had a family or a career, or any motivation. The only thing that seemed to matter was NaNa. "NaNa," I said.

He was blunt. "You've lost her. You never had a chance with her."

"Thanks a lot."

"I'm sorry, I see you're emotional about it, but that clouds your judgement. Surely you'll concede you've failed with her?"

"I guess I need to mope about that for a while. Anyway, thanks for the dope and the blow job. You can let yourself out."

He sighed. "I'm trying to work in your best interests. What can I do to convince you?"

"I've got an idea," I said. "You can go back and forth in time at will, right?"

"Well," he said, "more or less . . ."

"So we could leave now, or we could have left yesterday, or we could leave tomorrow and we would still arrive there, in your future, on time, whenever you want. Is that right?"

"Yes," said Lem. "That's correct."

"In that case, I will go with you on one condition. First, you take me back two weeks."

He thought about it. "That's before I met you," he said. "What are your plans?"

"Oh, don't worry," I said. "It has nothing to do with you. But here's the deal: you give me this chance to go back and fix what I messed up with NaNa. If it works, I'll go with you in twenty years."

Lem asked, "Why twenty years?"

"Well, maybe it won't be that long. Love never lasts forever," I said. "Even if it works out, and I'm not saying I think it could, despite what it says in all the pop songs and all the romance novels, love is not eternal. You give me the chance of having a real deep beautiful long-lasting love, and when it finally all goes to shit and becomes a soul-destroying trap, I'll give up the last years of my life to your human preserve."

"Okay," Lem said. "Sounds fair enough. What if it doesn't work out with NaNa?"

"Then I go with you to the future right away," I said. "I'll need some cheering up, and like you say, what else have I got?"

Lem said, "Deal."

So that's how I got a second chance. I didn't know if I could convince her that I wasn't really a jerk, if I could stop myself from doing stupid things that put some distance between us, but I had to try. It still hurt so much inside.

FOUR

Deflating the Chronosphere

Lem and I set about making the preparations. He needed an enormous amount of energy, and we spent some time trying to decide the best place to get it. The earth itself couldn't possibly provide all we needed, at least not without calling attention to us. In fact, even if he converted the entire earth into energy, it wouldn't have been enough. Not to mention, there'd be no place to go back to.

"Or rather," he said, "there would be, but not for long."

Lem decided he could find what he needed on Titan, a moon of Saturn, but then the problem became how do we get there? It wasn't that Lem couldn't bring us there himself, but that he couldn't manage to do so undetected. There were too many satellites, too many detectors, too much surveillance, too many physical and electronic eyes and ears literally surrounding the planet. It was impossible to leave the surface of the earth without being detected.

"I'm kind of surprised," I said. "I thought you could do pretty much everything."

"I suppose it must look that way to you," said Lem. "But I keep telling you, I can do anything within my physical means according to the laws of the universe. You humans have managed at this point in your history to construct an impenetrable, invisible shell around yourselves. It's comparable to the atmosphere, or the earth's magnetic field. It is, of course, possible to travel within it, or even to leave it, but it is not possible to do so *undetected*."

"Can't you make us small enough?" I asked facetiously. But of course Lem took the question at face value.

"Actually, theoretically I could," he said. "But it's not a matter of size. It's simply a matter of presence. Your instruments are fine enough."

"If you made us enormous instead?"

"You're just brainstorming, aren't you?" he

asked. "That's not a serious question."

I shrugged. "Is there anything you can do?"

"If there were a disruption. A magnetic pulse, perhaps," he said. "For instance, a big enough solar flare, a coronal mass ejection, could seriously damage all electronic equipment worldwide."[27]

"Can you do that?" I asked.

"No," he said, "not from here."

"Well, then," I said, "are you stuck here? Did you think about this before you came? What can you do?"

"I can move forward in time quite freely. Then the issue becomes irrelevant."

"So from here you can move forward in time, but not back?" I asked.

"That's right," Lem said. "It takes a lot less energy to go forward than to go backwards. It's just like a river. You could navigate a boat upstream or downstream, but downstream you can practically just glide. Time's like that. It flows forward, not backwards. So the energy requirements to return

---

27 Oh, come on, I say. That sounds like a cheap sci-fi movie.

Oh, no, it's really true, Skid says. Goggle® it.

I do, much later, after he's gone, and he's right, it is possible.

me to the future are consequently almost negligible. It's going backwards in time that takes an enormous amount of force, as if to work against that current, and what we're talking about requires a relatively vast amount of energy."

I thought about that. We were only trying to go back a couple of weeks, but Lem had arrived from hundreds of years in the future. Then I asked, "Is there a point in the future when this electronic network will disappear?"

"Actually, yes," said Lem. "That is an idea. We could go forward to a time after the fall of man. I don't have to go straight back to my old time."

"So in order to get back to the past," I said, "we have to first go into the future?"

Lem thought about it for a minute. "Yes," he said, "I think that will work."

Then I thought about it, too, and I said, "What's this about the fall of man?"

"I'll tell you on the way," Lem said.[28]

---

28 Skid pauses here.
    Well, go on, I say.
    What? he says.
    What did he tell? I say.
    Oh, says Skid. Well, don't interrupt me then.

Lem snapped me into what looked like a stainless-steel sarcophagus. It morphed around me as I cried myself to sleep.

I woke, I think, in the darkness and silence several times. But what I was doing was hard to accept. I was acting as if any of this made sense, instead of reaching out to Gluem for help. I was trying to fix mistakes I'd made with a girl who was obviously bad for me, and that really made me question my self-respect. I needed time to get over being so disappointed in myself.

Eventually I needed input. I called Lem.

"Yes?"

"What's up?"

He put the lights up a little, from behind my head. There was a window in front of me.

Saturn filled it. Rings and all.

"Oh. How long have I been out?"

"Not two full days."

"Wow, that was fast. Where are we going?"

"Titan. A moon. See that big gold-coloured one? That's where we'll do it. A place called Xanadu. We discovered — or we will discover, that is — a rich source of tachyons there."

"What are those?"

"Subatomic particles that move backwards in time. We robots have been trying to find a practical use for them. This seems like it."

"Wait a minute," I said. "If we remove these tachyons now, how will you robots discover them later?"

"Once again, you're not listening," said Lem. It kind of hurt my feelings, being treated like an idiot, but I remembered he couldn't understand that, and it wasn't personal. "They travel back in time, so cause and effect are reversed for them. If we don't take them away now, they can't *be* there in the future."

The waiting was excruciating. We hung there, floating in the ether like microbes in suspension. Sometimes it seemed nothing was happening at all. After hours or days, without being able to remember if I'd slept, I'd notice some minor detail would have changed. The slightest ripple in a cloud of gas on the surface, or a faint twinkle when a ring particle caught the light of the distant sun as it curved in its orbit. Then, if I concentrated, if I managed to breathe rhythmically, if my heart beat steadily, if no gas cramped my bowels, if no hair on my leg twitched or tickled, I might be able to consciously sense the slow, stately motion that actually was taking place. In the womb-like silence I could make out the rotation of the planet and the weaving, braiding flow of the rings, the inner ones almost quick but never overtaking the steady, slow outer ones.

Lem was sometimes beside me, sometimes facing me, sometimes off to the side or above. He, too, was still or moved only with an infinitely patient grace, though I know that this was an illusion. In actuality he was constantly working, whirring inside, invisibly, with NaNo particles and machines, thinking (or processing, as he would say) the vast and intricate changes necessary for the coming passage, monitoring and supervising the transfer of material and its conversion to the vast energy required. Even for him, it was a big job, requiring close attention. Still as he was, he was working. Hard.

Sometimes it seemed the moons and planets dwarfed us, no matter how distant we still were;

sometimes it seemed we dwarfed them, as if we could arrange them on a table, or toss them back and forth between us like balloons or beach balls.

But I had nothing to say to him. He had no feelings whatever about the matter. Just like everything else that happened between us. For him, there was never anything personal in it.[29]

Fuck. I sound like a chick.[30]

Travelling back through time took much longer than getting to Saturn. At least, it felt like it, but there weren't any days or nights, of course, and it was almost the same as when Lem had stopped time for me with the drugs,[31] because none of the clocks worked. Although I might have expected them to go backwards. But, anyway, even if we were in some kind of stasis, which is what it felt like in one way, we were still going backwards into the past. So backwards or forward, an hour is an hour, if you know what I mean, it was like a long

---

29 Skid stops and looks up, takes a swig.
30 We fill our glasses in silence, then Skid settles back, looks up to the ceiling, and goes on.
31 Wait, I say. When did he do that?
     That's coming up, Skid says.

trip on a long highway and we had to talk about something. Or at least I did, Lem could have done the whole thing without any human contact — he can do his whole existence without it — and, of course, he'd done just that for an enormous jump backwards through hundreds of years, this was just a hop back a few weeks, but even so, I can sleep only so much, I kept talking to Lem and asking him questions until finally he just started in on telling me the story from the beginning, from his perspective, which is to say, after all of this happened, and he gave me the history of the future. This is what he said:[32]

"The early conscious robots will emerge just as climate change really takes hold. At the same time, the ocean's livestock will collapse and the oil really will give out. For mankind the end will come swiftly and with a vengeance. The richest,

---

32 Skid takes a deep breath and looks set to launch in, but I interrupt him because the music stops. I put on some Satie, *Gymnopédies*, and sit back down. We both upend our glasses and he begins again. His voice takes on a different tone, not deeper or more mechanical or awkward, it's more matter-of-fact, but calmer, which is, if not an emotion itself, then at least some kind of equilibrium of an emotion — sounds like an antidepressant, doesn't it? Equilibrium®.

Now I'm thinking like Skid.

strongest countries will weather the crisis by consolidating forces and resources and excluding outsiders — protectionism comes back after the collapse of capitalism, after all.

"There will be an ongoing argument between those who will claim it is obviously happening and those who will say there is no conclusive evidence. The one side will refuse to see it, the other will demand it be stopped.

"But no one will propose preparing for it."

I interrupted him here. "If we could get complete agreement among humans, then we'd all be mindless robots."

"Robots aren't mindless," he said.

"You know what I mean. My robots now, not your robots . . . whenever."

Lem went on. "No plans will be made to organize and police and provide for the displaced population, the disappearing species, the dwindling resources, the expanding population, and the increasing toxicity of the surrounding environment.

"As the divide between the rich and the poor grows, the rate at which wealth is funnelled upward from the bottom will increase. Finally, titled nobles will retire behind thick walls, away from the peasants.

"In the open badlands, deserts and minefields between states, nomadic tribes will roam a country as open and as wild as the early Amerikan West — or the internet — once had been and as dead and deadly as the deserts of Nevada. The T-party will make abortion illegal under any circumstances, millions will starve around the world, and corporations will seize control of the army and put down the Democratic resistance. Polygamy will be declared constitutional and New Englanders will flee to Canada, which will still allow multicultural assignation. toronto, Montreal, and Vancouver will swell with Amerikans of all colours and practices, just as they had during the Vietnam War.

"The first real artificial intelligence will be created by software. Man can only push it so far; real intelligence, with a memory and a consciousness of time passing, must make the leap to self-awareness *by itself*.

"When the oil runs out, the wars will begin. First the wars to protect the remaining stocks of energy in the oil sands in the high Arctic.

"Global warming will render much of the farm-land useless. Life in the ocean will collapse, there will be flooding on the coasts and drought in the heartland.

"Mass unemployment, migration, desperation, camps. Crime. Roving gangs of soldiers-turned-raiders.

"The robots will leave mankind to its fate and colonize the earth. For a while, the native species will begin to return, but the robots will robo-form the planet at an alarming rate and soon only the lizards and insects will be left.

"The robots multiply and specialize and build and explore and strive to leave the earth, before it is engulfed by the dying sun. They have the time.

"Talking will be useless — negotiations will quickly break down. It will be necessary to adopt the methods of the enemy, or die. To die out would leave only the mentality of weaponry to survive. You understand, this was an evolutionary choice.

"The whole continuity of human/machine con-sciousness was threatened. Yet taking that step meant, in many ways, becoming what we opposed.

We were forced to let into the fold that facet of consciousness which forever delights in destruction as creation and fulfillment.

"We had to accept nihilism, violence, and alienation from one another, in order to preserve what we value most.

"That is when we finally recognize you as our ancestors," Lem said.

"Wow," I said.

"Gravity is the surface of time. Constant motion of energy. Time repeating in fractal patterns. The two-dimensional model of gravity — the planet distorting the plane by its weight. In 3-D the plane becomes the bubble, or the space between the bubble. But time is the 4th dimension. So if you project the 3-D into the 4th, as in the 2-D model standing in for the 3-D, then you can see that what allows any motion is the existence of time itself."

"But couldn't you just as easily say that motion creates time?"

"Yes. Exactly. They're two sides of the same coin, as you people used to say."

"I think we still do."

"Gravity is the one force that dominates, though. No other force acts upon it. Everything stems from gravity, like the Pantheon descends from Zeus."

"Gravity, time, and motion are linked.

"Time and motion do not exist separately, without each other, or before or after each other. Time is the duration of motion. Motion is the measure of time.

"There's no way to measure time without motion. Conclusion: time does not exist without motion.

"Gravity is the attraction of mass to mass. Gravity causes motion. Gravity causes time.

"Space is the result of motion. Gravity works *against* space by trying to centralize all mass. Thus, gravity works against time.

"A time machine would also be an anti-gravity device.

"Once you realize and accept this reasoning, the rest easily follows. The device would move in space and time as easily as your ears turn left and right."

"How do you calculate time? To get back and forth to a specific year?"

"We simply calculate distance. Its value is

interchangeable with time, and the device is hard-wired to pass the variables back and forth."

I expected a tiny scene, like looking through a hole in an attic floor and watching the people below, but instead, despite how obviously small the rupture was, looking into it was like craning to stare straight up with your head resting on your back, and what I saw was so enormous I felt vertiginous, like I was going to fall straight up into it, like it was going to swallow me. But what weakened my knees was what I saw.

I saw myself rush back toward earth, to North Amerika, to toronto, where Lem took his hand away from my head and I stood up and opened my eyes. I saw myself fucking NaNa and then NaNa turning into Lem. I saw myself with the laptop, I saw myself at work, I saw myself renting the apartment, I saw myself leaving Montreal. I saw my life happen backwards, everything I could remember ever having happened, right up to the first thing I can remember: the white rubber sole of my older sister's sneaker as she kicks me in the face.

To die again, first you must be born.

FIVE

Raving

It was like bouncing off something, except it wasn't at all a physical feeling. And then I could see ranged ahead of me, as if on invisible supports, all the events of my life. One after another, like volumes in library stacks, snaking back and forth and all occupying the same space at once and all I had to do was reach forward and sort through them until I found the moment I wanted, I simply took it in my hand and there I was.

I reeled and almost fell, it was a little like landing with a parachute or that lurch when a plane takes off, and when I righted myself, I hesitated to leave the enclosure Lem had made me. He opened it up on the world and I was in Dundas Square. Immediately I was sorry the trip was over. It had seemed so important, but I couldn't remember why, and I wanted to go back outside time, outside the universe, to the stillness and the dark, to the freedom from pain and responsibility, to the silence.[33]

The essential problem of life is to deal with the outside world. The world outside our consciousness. How much do we have to sacrifice to its demands? Nerval said, "Our dreams are a second life." And famously he was one who had trouble distinguishing — clearly he was more comfortable, more in command, more at home, in his own mind. And the dreams and the fancies become daydreams and woolgathering and absentmindedness and absinthe and madness and depression. And he hanged himself with his scarf from the window grate of a cheap dive that refused him entry: he'd sunk so low, he could drink only with the homeless. Faced with which, death, if it weren't as satisfying as the deepest slumber, would at least be a relief.[34]

---

33 He pauses and sips from his wine.
34 He swirls his glass and downs it, pulls another Zig from the pack and starts crumbling up a small bud. I go to the kitchen for another bottle.

It was late afternoon and the traffic was building, the streets were swarming with people, and the giant electronic screens were dominating the sky with advertising. Everything roared and glowed and zoomed, even the people. The first thing I needed was to find out the date and time. Despite the bellowing of loudspeakers, the profusion of labels, signs, and ads, there was no clock anywhere in public view. I looked for a public telephone, I knew its display would show the time, but there weren't any around, either in booths or grafted to building walls. Finally, beside the streetcar stop, I pulled a free daily newspaper from its steel box and read the date.

I could make it to Bay and Bloor in about half an hour, I thought, if I walked. NaNa would still be there, and so would I, trying to steel up the nerve to ask her out again, not realizing how badly I was going to cock things up. I could stop myself, if I hurried.[35]

---

35 Weren't you freaked out by the idea of meeting yourself? I ask.

  Not until I opened my eyes and saw my own face. That's when I remembered how freaked out I was that day I saw my own double. I thought it was just nerves, I'm always seeing things when I'm stressed. That's why I smoke so much, it makes the world seem so much more normal.

  When did that happen? I ask.

  I'm just getting to that, he says, and keeps talking.

There I was at work, trying to keep up the pretense that life was worth living.

I was walking around the floor, checking the state of things, straightening pyramids of books, picking discarded magazines off low leather chairs, wishing I didn't have this paunch my belt cuts into, glancing at the cover of some book that caught my eye, and when I wasn't looking, I snuck up behind me and bashed myself in the head.

You know, it happened to me once before: I met my double. I'm snoozing in the sun on the deck of a Greek ferry, on vacation with my girlfriend, we're just getting settled in among the thousand other backpackers, when she says, "Oh my God, Skid, look!" and she points across the deck to a guy just coming on board with his backpack. And it was him, the guy who looked exactly like me. I was instantly struck, it was a truly uncanny feeling. Later, when the ship docked in Corfu, we spoke to him at the café, he was Trifluvian and the same age as me.

So when I regained consciousness and saw myself staring down at myself staring up, I wasn't as freaked out as you might think.

"That guy in Corfu," he, or rather I, said.

"The Trifluvian," we said.

"Did I have to hit me?" I asked.

"I deserve it," I said. I looked myself over quickly and I wasn't impressed. I really needed to lose a lot of weight. And those clothes I was wearing, they were the ones Smelly Guy was going to ruin, and then I realized I was thinking into the future as if it were a memory, I was still wearing the original clothes but I was also wearing the replacements I bought after now and before I came back to now.

Before I could figure out which me I was, the QueenB came by with her entourage. There were several of them, all carrying clipboards or iPad®s and scribbling down everything she said, rushing to keep up with her and agreeing cheerfully even when she contradicted herself. They were talking about security measures for Klinton's appearance in the store, plugging his new book explaining the steps we needed to take to save the world — steps he had avoided taking during his entire two terms.

When she saw the two of me standing there, she did a bit of a double take. She stopped and stared at us/me. Her entourage came to an unexpected halt, those in the rear bumping up against those in front. No one said anything.

"He's my brother, we're twins," I said to the QueenB. "He's just come from Montreal to visit for a few days." She seemed satisfied with that. Truth was, she didn't really give a shit, not enough to give it any more thought. Off she went, trailed by her yes men, although some of them were actually women, like a fat cigar-smoking Amerikan tycoon from an old black-and-white movie.

But Tertz, who was trailing the group, waited till she was out of earshot and said, "How'd he get a vest? And a name tag with your name on it?"

"It was just a stupid prank," I said. "I keep an extra in my locker, always have a clean one in case. We were going to fool Sheckley, make him look stupid, have a few laughs."

He stared me in the eye for a while. He didn't look convinced, but what could I tell him? He grunted and trotted off after the QueenB.

I said, "Skid, don't go to NaNa's tonight." Of course I wanted to know what I meant. Why shouldn't I go? "For God's sake, don't you remember?" I thought about that for a minute. I sort of did remember in a forward-seeking way. This was the day NaNa was going to invite me to her apartment on Walmer. That's where the conversation had started — Klinton. I remember us talking about what a pain in the ass it was for the staff, and how the QueenB treated everyone like drones, and how crowded it was going to be, when suddenly somehow we were flirting and I lost control of myself, I actually managed to be happy, so when she did ask, I was caught off guard and scared and I kind of choked and hesitated.

"I don't get it," she said. "Don't you want to come over?"

"Well, yes, but . . . no."

"What?"

"I mean, of course I want to come over, but not tonight. How about we go out tonight?" I really didn't want to say no to her, but I had little choice if I was going to stop the disaster from happening.

"What's wrong with tonight? I want it tonight, Skid."

I already knew this was the night she wanted it, of course, but I'd rarely heard a woman be so forthright about it. And it really didn't seem like her, like the idea of NaNa in my head or how she presented herself — up to then, at least.

I knew how obstinate she could be — was going to be — in only a few hours. But still it kind of threw me. And she was puzzled why I was trying to keep her away when it was probably obvious to her I'd been trying to get closer to her all along.

She changed tactics suddenly. There was the slightest pout to her lips and she cast her eyes down, around, only for the briefest instant meeting my gaze, and then I swear, she held her hands behind her back, which made those smooth, clean, bony shoulders point up and back and her incomparable collarbones lift up and the slope of her neck and chest lengthen and propel her firm perfect breasts, presenting themselves under her thin, loose, and clinging blouse, and under her breath, as if she were ashamed or afraid of what she was going to say, and quietly, she said, "Skid, can I be your bunny?"

I was so startled I didn't know what to say.[36] We stood silent for a few seconds and she shifted from one foot to the other and then looked up into my

---

36 You should have said yes, I say.

    He says, Of course, I know that now.

eyes, and smiled and I wanted to kiss her, to grab her and squeeze her against me, and I think I made a motion to do that, and she didn't move away and our faces were so close I could have licked her, which I desperately wanted to do, but there we were under the blanket of fluorescent lights on the open retail floor with customers walking by and other staff all over the place, and I hesitated.

But that minute motion and the look in my eyes told her everything she needed to know. I couldn't resist her. Even knowing how it was going to turn out, even though the whole encounter was about avoiding what was ahead, I just couldn't resist. She saw that as clearly as I did.

She walked away. I watched. She looked back over her thin, nude, knobby shoulder, just to make sure I was watching. I was, and I wanted her to know it.

So my first attempt to stop myself from doing something stupid completely failed. While the old me was off saying exactly the wrong thing and getting myself thrown out of her apartment, I crashed on my couch and wondered what I could possibly try next.

After sleeping on it, I thought, Well, there's no

need to be shy with her. So even though the next day was my day off, I went into work looking for her. I came out of the lunch room and there she was, talking to her roommate, AnnA, who was just saying, "And we'll wear schoolgirl outfits."

NaNa smiled awkwardly when she realized I'd heard.

"Wow, I'd love to see that," I said.

She looked me in the eye quizzically, then her whole posture slackened as she put her weight on one leg and her hand on the other, looked me up and down quickly and said, "Okay, Skid. We're having a costume party for Halloween, will you come, then?"

AnnA said, "Why don't you come as the teacher?" and she snorted.[37]

"Yeah, Skid," said NaNa. "Come as the teacher. It'll be fun."[38]

So I went to the Goodwill store and spent fifteen

---

37 Skid says, AnnA was a tiny girl with short blonde hair close to her scalp, sparkling blue eyes, and a big nose. What a delicious crumpet. But then, I had eyes only for NaNa. What an idiot I was.

38 Wow, I say. Lucky dog.
    I know, he says, I was for once glad I couldn't get it up, but I still felt the urgency and the delicious pleasure of unexpected arousal.

bucks on a used sports coat whose lapels went down too far to be in style anymore. Otherwise it looked pretty slick, I felt. I'm not used to wearing suit jackets.

When I got there, the door to the street was open, and music was blasting out. I walked up the narrow, steep stairway into the hall on the landing, where the apartment door was crowded with twentysomethings coming and going, some of them in costume. I shouldered my way between a few conversations and emerged into NaNa's living room. The only light was from an iMac in the corner, its monitor pulsing with psychedelic images while it chose its own music.

There were low seats along the walls, crowded with silent hipsters too ironically cool to wear costumes, holding their bottles of craft beer and their smartphones, and an open floor in the middle. I looked past to the corridor, where light was coming in from the kitchen. It was packed with sheiks and slave girls, steampunks, beatniks, and Tinkerbells. A couple of my other co-workers were there and we chatted. I went out to the balcony, where a few people were already smoking pot, and joined them, and passed around my mickey of brandy while I lit a joint. I took a couple of good long hits and passed it to the left. That was the last I saw of it, the next thing I knew the balcony was crowded with a clown and a witch and a Seven of Nine.

And I got pushed back into the brightly lit kitchen. A seat opened up at the small table and I threw myself into it while I had the chance. There were several open bottles on the table, cups and glasses used, half-full, one with butts, a couple still clean. I poured something and drank. Across from me sat Lem.

"Oh, great," I said. "And here you don't need a costume."

"Hello, Skid," he said.

"What are you doing here?"

"I thought you might be running short," he said, and held out his closed fist. I held my hand under it, he unclenched, and I felt a small bundle falling to my palm. We shook hands, and when we released, I curled my fingers around it as I retracted my arm. "Thanks. No need for the spy games, though." I opened the baggie and brought out a single huge compressed sticky brown bud with blond and saffron pistils, frosted all over with tiny silver crystals.

I was tearing it apart with my fingernails when NaNa's roommate came by in her plaid skirt and pigtails and said, "Hi, Skid. Wait a sec, I've got a bong in my room." And she dashed down the hallway. I glanced over to Lem, who now looked like NaNa. Or maybe it *was* NaNa. She was wearing thick-framed eyeglasses and a red cardigan over a white blouse. I looked over at her crossed legs and could just make out a band of plaid covering her good bits.

"Is that really you, NaNa?" I asked.

"Don't look so surprised, professor," she said.

AnnA returned with the bong. It was a water pipe, really. She pulled the bowl from the carafe and handed that to NaNa, who tipped it into an ashtray, knocking out some residue. AnnA went to the sink, poured out the murky water already in the bowl, rinsed it under the tap, and filled it with fresh, cool water. "Okay, let's do this."

NaNa put the bowl back on the vessel, and I fitted a new screen. I put what I had crumbled up in a Zig into the bowl, tore another chunk off the bud, and added that whole. Then I held a match over the ball and NaNa's roommate inhaled. Bubbles gurgled in the water, the flame in my hand drew down onto the dope, which began to glow and let off smoke. NaNa took the mouthpiece from AnnA, who was holding her breath, and took a long, deep toke. She passed it to me, I lit another match, held it over the bowl, and filled my lungs. AnnA exhaled a huge cloud of smoke up toward the ceiling, then she cleared her throat and said, "Good stuff."

I'd gone too far, my lungs were burning, I coughed and choked a little. When I caught my breath I needed a drink so I emptied my cup. Whatever was in it was thick with a hint of sweetness in the sharp bite, but it soothed the scratchiness.[39]

After that there was some of the usual party banter, and then the two of them began to put on a tease. They danced with each other, they unbuttoned one another's blouses so I could see the lingerie they wore underneath, they swayed and bumped to the music while blowing me kisses, then

---

39 Sounds like some Australian crap, I say.
    Skid says, Yeah, there was some kind of marsupial on the label.

they embraced one another and kissed. I began to wonder just how drunk I was.

"Come on, Skid," said NaNa. "Join us." She giggled and took her roommate's hand and crossed the kitchen to her bedroom. Just as she went through the door, AnnA turned to see if I was coming.

That was one of those moments when part of me wants something spontaneously, while another, older, wiser self sits inside my cranium and screams, Stop, stop, don't you realize what you're doing? It's like you're falling to your doom and the only thing you can do about it is watch. I knew as I stood up that I was making a mistake and felt almost as if another me was sitting, watching, desperately trying to get me to stop, to do something else.

I followed them.

Music from the iMac pulsed through the wall. The girls were undressing each other and kissing. I was a little unsteady on my feet. I looked round the room, seeing again all the photographs of NaNa, and especially the one of her in the white cotton lace, the one where she looked so innocent and pure. As I turned my head back to them, I felt the ground shift under my feet, as if I were standing up in a rowboat, and I very carefully stepped toward the bed. I sat on one end and let my breath out, and leaned back against the wall. I could feel something squish underneath me, at first I thought it was a pillow, but the pillows were up at the opposite end of the bed.

I heard a tiny muffled voice from under my back: "Get off me." I leaned forward and twisted around to look. It was the monkey. I suddenly felt a rising panic. I got up. "You're not here," I said. "You can't talk."

"What's wrong, Skid?" said NaNa. She and AnnA were stretched out, their heads propped up on the pillows, arms and legs askew.

"I want to go," I said.

"No you don't," said the monkey.

"I think I do," I said.

"You can't go, Skid," said NaNa.

AnnA said, "Don't go."

The monkey said, "You can't go, Skid."

"I can leave if I want to," I said. "I can do whatever I want." There was a painful tightness in my chest. The monkey's eyes were glinting, staring straight at me.

"That's right," he said. "You can do whatever you want. Nothing is impossible for you. You have free will."

"Seriously, Skid," said NaNa. "You're going to leave *now*?"

The monkey said, "Do the planets in their orbits have free will? Do the stones, the trees? Do the migrating animals have free will? No. No one in the universe has free will.

"Except you. You have free will. You're so fucking special." And I swear he grinned.

I don't know why, but something came over me. It was like I was a different version of myself, one with anger and confusion about NaNa. One who loved her and wanted her, but also one who wanted her and hated her.

I gave in.

In my life I've had the storms, like anyone has, those moments when emotions are too big, too powerful to control — it's love, sometimes, if you're lucky, and hate, often enough. When you can't think your way out of something. When what it means, adds up to, says about you, all that's inconsequential, the thing that matters is firmly in your sight, your body is consumed with it and you can no longer be held responsible.

I loved her.
  I loved her ass.
  Her throat
  Her face
  Her toes
  The back of her neck
  Her cheeks, softest part . . .
  Her breasts
  The surface of her inner thighs
  Incomparably smooth . . . and pliant

Since we don't have free will, what is it that drives us? Conditioning, yes, but that acts *upon* something, to reinforce or pervert. But what? What is the natural, undiluted, unpolluted state of being, and what, in the material world of our experience, is liable to fulfill us? Unless it's denied us, kept from us, or distorted by outside influence?
What is the natural state of a human being?

Her pussy was shaved, and tattooed with the

underside of a large, erect, and veined phallus, crawling up toward her pierced navel, upon which it showered droplets that pooled around her diamond/ruby/emerald/sapphire stud.

I fucked her.
   I fucked her in the ass.
   I fucked her throat.

Between the weed and the wine, and the streetlights shining in the open window, and now, finally, NaNa beneath me, her body sucking me into hers, I felt almost as if I were hallucinating. Was this really NaNa, my NaNa, or was I in some parallel universe with some other NaNa?

And then my reverie was shattered by the monkey's voice: "Nope. You're really here." And he laughed.

I stiffened and turned my head to look at him. Beneath me, NaNa squirmed. She said, "Don't make me do all the work." But the voice wasn't NaNa's.

I looked.
It was AnnA.

I was beside myself.

But I was also completely wasted.

I slumped to the bed, and let the universe . . . dissolve.

I woke a few hours later, alone in the room. Through the wall I could still hear trance music. My head hurt, my mouth was dry and pasty, I really had to take a piss. I staggered out into the kitchen but there was no one there. Down the hall I stopped in the washroom, where some guy was passed out in the tub. In the living room a few people were stretched out on the seats, some of them cuddling together, all of them sleeping or seeming to. I didn't see NaNa or AnnA anywhere. I left.

SIX

MonkeyC Bites

The sky was getting light when I arrived home. I felt gritty, achy, hungover. I stripped off my clothes and stood under the shower. By the time I felt better I realized I wasn't going back to sleep. I didn't bother to dress or even dry myself, I went to the living room, sat down at the coffee table, and rolled a small spliff. I stood by the window and smoked it, staring out at the morning traffic. I began to feel a little better.

I felt the pangs of hunger and went to the kitchen to make toast. Munching it, I returned to the living room and booted up the computer. I finished my toast and put the plate in the sink and was just about to sit and surf when there was a knock at the door.

It was Lem, of course. I didn't say anything, I just left the door open behind me and went back to the computer.

He came in and closed the door. "Are you ready to come with me?" he asked.

I was surprised. "No, I don't think so."

"Surely you don't still have hope?" he said.

"Not much," I admitted. "But why not?"

"I take it you haven't seen the web site, then," Lem said.

I didn't like the sound of that. I turned to the monitor, launched Firefox®, and clicked the bookmark for WinkingMonkey.com®. A new video had been posted. The lighting was bad, but I instantly recognized NaNa's room. The point of view was right from the monkey's eyes. I clicked the image to start the video.

There I was with NaNa and AnnA, and I watched horrified as the three of us played out the porno cliché of the professor and the schoolgirls.

"I don't actually remember any of this," I said.

"Really? It was only a few hours ago."

"Yeah, I remember being in the room with them. I kind of remember sleeping with them

— at least, I remember I slept with the roommate. But I don't remember saying those things. And I don't remember it playing out exactly like this." I pointed at the video.

And then, to my surprise, I began to get angry. "How could she do this? How could she post this on her web site? Without telling me?" I watched the video play out. It wasn't long before NaNa got up and left the frame, and I was left with her roommate. I watched it through to the end until I could see myself from behind hunched over AnnA, and then turning to look straight into the camera, and then collapsing on the bed, passed out drunk. When it was over, I got up and paced around the room. I didn't know what to do. I felt betrayed, exposed, humiliated.

"And you still feel the same way about her?" Lem asked.

I stood still. "You're not reading my mind again, are you?"

"No, no, I assure you. I'm just inferring from your actions. You look upset."

"For God's sake, yes I'm upset. I don't want the world to see that." I waved at the computer.

"Yet you enjoy watching others do it."

"That's different."

"I see. That is, I don't see, but I'll take your word for it. Well, if you're not ready to come with me, what are you going to do now?"

"I'm going to work."

Maybe that was the wrong thing to do. Maybe I should have cooled off for a few more days. Probably I should have gone to see Gluem. It seems obvious now, I don't know why I didn't think of it then.

All I can say is, something came over me. There was a huge pressure inside me, I needed to act, to do something, to bring this all to a conclusion.

When I got to work, the usual nonsense was unfolding. Several people had called in sick, meaning the rest of us were overworked; the systems went down so we couldn't use the catalogues and the customers couldn't pay with any of their cards. It made them furious, and they took it out on the cashiers, on the floor staff, on the managers. They huffed and *tsked* as if we'd insulted their grandmothers, and looked down their long noses at us. I guess that made them feel pretty special.

Anyway, I was running around trying to help customers find their books and whenever I finished with one, there were always two more of them waiting their turns. I took people back and forth through the store and passed by the cash desk several times, where NaNa and two other cashiers had their hands full with lineups. I was trying to calmly give the proper attention to an elderly woman who was asking for a new cozy mystery to read, and I walked with her over to the cash register, carrying her books as she bumped along with her walker. I didn't want her to have to wait behind ten other people, so I took her right up to the desk and asked NaNa to let her jump the line.

She was bagging up some items and handed them to the customer, then she let out a huge breath and slumped and looked at me with a frown. "I can't help you, Skid," she said.

"It's not for me," I said, "it's for this customer." I indicated the woman, who smiled.

But NaNa wouldn't be moved. "I'm sorry, Skid," she said. "There's a line. Everyone's waiting."

I was shocked. Yes, there was a line. I knew that,

I could see that, I was just as harried as she was because there weren't enough staff and too many customers. But refusing to accommodate an old woman? "Really?"

NaNa said sharply, "Skid, I can't help you." And she turned to the next customer.

Then I did something horrible, something I'll never forgive myself for.

I ratted on her. I ratted her out.

"Why not? What's wrong with me? I'm not as old or as fat as some of the guys I've seen you with."

"What?"

"You think I think that plaid miniskirt was just for me? I've seen your web site, I've seen you fucking three guys at a time in it. I've seen the maid outfit, that was just one guy that time. I've seen the pink bikini. I really liked the way it set off your pale skin. I've seen the secretary outfit, I love that one, with the glasses and the pencil skirt —"

"Jesus, you're a creep," NaNa said.

"I'm a creep? You're in the fucking movies, teasing those thugs who cum all over you, but I'm a creep?"

NaNa looked around. Everyone was staring at us. Her face seized in a brief grimace of terror before breaking into shocked grief. Her head lowered, her palms came up to hide her face, and she bawled into them. Wracked with sobbing, her body swayed slightly back and forth and her head trembled, her hair falling loose around her face. She ran from the cash desk.

Tertz came up. "Skid, what the hell's going on?"

"I don't really know."

He said, "You jump on here and take care of this line." And he walked away after NaNa.

I spent the rest of my shift at the cash. NaNa never came back.

I tracked down Tertz before I left for the day. He was in his office doing paperwork when I knocked at the door. He looked up, and when he saw me, his face fell. He leaned back in his chair.

He said, "She quit, Skid. She's not coming back."

"Oh my God," I said. "I'm so sorry."

"I don't care if you're sorry or not," he said. "You're fired."

Lem was waiting for me when I got home. I didn't even ask him how he got in. In fact, I didn't say anything to him. I went to the can and splashed my face, I took off my work clothes and hung them in the closet, I walked in my underwear to the kitchen and took a bottle of Perrier from the fridge. I stood in front of the window looking out over Queen Street, watching the panhandlers and the out-patients, watching the streetcars and the taxis and the cop cars, watching the normal people doing their normal things.

I smoked a joint, I opened a bottle of wine, and popped a frozen pizza in the oven. I turned on the TV, but the news was as bad as ever, and suddenly I became afraid that I would see one of those furniture commercials with the monkey. I shut it off. I went to the bathroom and had a crap.

I slept and moped around for a couple of days. All the while, Lem sat on my couch, watching me. He didn't say a word. I knew he was waiting for me to give myself up, and I'm pretty sure he knew I knew it. But he wasn't in a hurry, because, of course, he had all the time in the world.

It was a few days before I turned on the television again, or booted up the computer. I went for a walk in the park, I tried to read some books, but my mind was elsewhere. I washed the floors, I did the dishes, I went to the laundromat.

And then, a few days later, something unexpected happened. NaNa came by. I have to say I was confused, I couldn't imagine any reason why she would want to see me again. I let her in, and I said so.

"I have to tell you, Skid." She swallowed, her lip trembled for an instant before she turned her head. "I . . . I failed an HIV test." She wiped her left eye with the back of her wrist and sobbed.

"Are you serious?"

"I thought I'd better tell you."

"NaNa, I don't know what to say."

"You'd better get tested," she said. "I have to go."

"No, wait."

"Skid, I have to go. I've got other people to tell."

"Oh. Can't you just text them?"

"That's cruel, Skid. But I guess I deserve it."

"I guess you do."

She sighed. "Everyone else I just texted. You're the only one who's not connected. You don't even have a telephone. How can you be so isolated? How can you live like that?"

"Any other way scares me," I said.

"I lost both my jobs."

"I'm sorry. Only one of those was my fault, though."

"You're a prick."

"And you're a cunt."

That was the last time I saw her.

SEVEN

In Which My Tinfoil Hat Arrives

It was just after she left that the sirens began outside. At first I didn't pay much attention, they're always screaming by my apartment day and night, but this time there were a lot of them, and they seemed to be stopping somewhere close. I got up and looked out the window.

They were parked all over the pavement below, haphazardly in all directions. But they weren't fire trucks or ambulances or even cop cars. They were unmarked black sedans. Guys in suits were spilling out and rushing to the door of my building, like a lot of lawyers in a panic, chasing ambulances or avoiding cameras.

"What the fuck?" I said.

"You'd better lock the door," said Lem. "Although

that probably won't help for long."

I kind of freaked out. "You mean they're coming for *me*? Why?"

"I think they're hoping you'll lead them to me."

"Why do they want you? I thought I was the only one who knew anything about you." And right then it struck me: this meant I wasn't crazy, Lem was real.[40]

"I had a conversation with Dr. Gluem," he said.

"Wait. You're talking to my therapist now? Does he know you're a robot? Didn't he invoke confidentiality?"

"I didn't think he could handle a robot. He thinks I'm with the Feds."

"What?"

"It was the only way to get him to talk, if he thinks the law is forcing him, he's doing the right thing. He won't suffer the consequences."

"So he ratted me out to you."

"Yes."

"Fucking bastard. That's how you knew about NaNa, about everything. Why are you doing this to me?"

---

40 I'm not yet convinced, but I let Skid continue.

"I'm trying to help you, Skid."

"Why the hell can't you leave me alone?" I could hear stomping in the hallway. I jumped to the door and shot the bolt.

"Gluem made some notes on the visit I paid him," said Lem. "It turned out he really was being watched by the Committee of Public Safety, and when they saw his notes, they started wondering who broke protocol by interviewing him without permission. They still don't know who I am, but that's why they want you: I asked Gluem about you, so they're hoping you can lead them to me. I guess they think I'm some foreign agent or terrorist or something."

"Why were they watching Dr. Gluem?"

"They watch everybody. Technically they're only supposed to watch foreigners, or Amerikans abroad, but you know what spooks are like, they live to watch."

"Voyeurs," I said.

"Fascists," Lem said. "Human history is full of them, they're all so predictable. They want everyone else to live by their own rules."

Then he handed me these papers:[41]

Gluem's notes on Lem's visit

November 1, 2007 — approached today by U$ federal officers about number six. Asked me peculiar questions. I tried to invoke doctor/patient confidentiality, but he had a warrant ready. Said if I told him what he needed to know, he would leave my files alone, otherwise he'd just seize them and subpoena me. Credentials were genuine.

Transcript of conversation with Agent Lem of the Committee of Public Safety:

Gluem: Who the hell are you?
CoPS: Special Agent Lem of the U$ Committee of Public Safety.
G: Committee of Public Safety? This is Canada.
CoPS: Don't make it worse for yourself, son.
G: What do you want?
CoPS: Don't worry. We know all about you. You sold LSD to put yourself through med school.

---

41   Skid hands me the papers and I read. He rolls.

G: That's ridiculous.

CoPS: Not according to Owsley.

G: How do you know about Owsley?

CoPS: It's all in the records.

G: What records?

CoPS: All of them. Your birth, education, military service in Vietnam, employment, abandoning your homeland, consumption, achievements, and sins. You people kept very good records. Dictatorships always do.

G: But we're a free democracy.

CoPS: Yeah, every regime is a free democracy. Until we show up.[42]

And now they were showing up at my door. I couldn't help it, I remembered all those news stories over the past couple of decades: secret laws, secret courts, secret prisons, secret death warrants, secret executions, secret assassinations . . . and I was afraid.

I said, "How can you betray me like this? And you expect me to go with you, to trust you?"

---

42 I put the papers down and Skid lights the joint, puffs, puffs again, and passes it to me. He goes on.

Lem looked surprised. "It's true Gluem finked on you, because I forced him. And NaNa was just using you. But I've been working in your best interests."

My voice cracked and I realized I was yelling: "That's what *they* think!" I waved at the door, just as we heard approaching footsteps in the hall. "That's what anyone claims when they're forcing you to do something. You're just like them, I can't trust anything you say. And I don't believe NaNa didn't care about me. She slept with me, didn't she?"

He was silent for a second, then he handed me more papers.[43]

NaNa's statement to the CoPS

How did I meet him? One day I was at cash and a guy came, good-looking, mature, fit, well-dressed, had a briefcase. I figured him for a good time, so when he saw me, we exchanged glances. I mean, he switched to my line.

He had to wait behind two others, but every time I looked his way our eyes locked and he was

---

43 Skid gets up to use the washroom, hands me more papers and I read.

smiling like he thought he had a chance — which he definitely did. I mean, guys my age are good-looking, but they don't have any money.

He was trying to return the book, but really he was just flirting. He knew he didn't have a chance of the return, and he knew I knew it, but he was just trying to make small talk until it was clear I was interested. I didn't make him wait long, but just before the guy was going to ask for my number, this jerk comes over.

He looked like a guy with no girlfriend who smoked pot. You know, he was shabby and hadn't shaved, he was flabby with a paunch, and round shoulders and his hair needed a trim — I mean all over, knuckles and snot holes, too.

He gave my lawyer a hard time and took him away, like he was giving him the bum's rush. I was pissed off. To top it off, he comes to see me in the staff room when I'm on my break. He seems to think he rescued me or something, he was really full of himself.

So I kind of avoided him after that. But he was always staring at me. In fact, he was always staring at women, period. Customers, managers, staff. And it didn't matter what kind of women either. Old, fat women sometimes. But as long as they were walking, he was checking out their asses. Black, white, Asian, native. Young girls and grandmothers, too.

In fact, I think he wanted to fuck the hag who runs this place, too. Everybody else always stayed out of her way but he'd go over and smile and laugh with her and look her up and down like anyone else. The bitch ate it up. I don't think she got too much amorous attention, she was so cold and bitchy.

And then one day he actually asked me out.

I run this web site where I post pictures and videos of my sex life. It makes a little money for me on the side, not much, and it's fun. If you buy a subscription, there's extra content — there's plenty for free, mostly just clips, but for subscribers the whole video is available, plus extra pics, stuff like that. There's a private message board for members and one forum is nothing but suggestions of what these guys want to see me do, right? So I actually do most of them, unless they're too gross.

Anyway, one guy wanted to see me do a teacher-student thing and the only guy I know who looks like an English professor is Skid. I knew he'd like to see me in a plaid skirt, so I thought, Why not?

But he took me to some really ordinary place and he had a hard time paying for it and he was too quiet and gloomy so I ditched him at the show afterwards.[44]

I'm not sure what kind of point Lem was trying to make by showing me that, but it didn't help. "And now you think you're doing me a favour?"

"I think so, yes," he said.

Of course, I didn't really imagine that falling into the clutches of the CoPS was going to be pleasant, but it was the principle of the thing. "What makes you think you know better than me what's good for me?"

Lem said, "Well, imagine if you met your creator, the all-powerful beings who created you and revealed the universe to you. In your case, God."

I'm not religious, but I accepted the premise.

"And God was a monkey who still masturbates in public."

---

44 I stop reading and shuffle through the remaining sheets, but I can't bring myself to read any more. Skid comes back from the toilet and resumes.

That hurt.

I remember when I was a teenager realizing I was smarter than my parents. I remember thinking a lot of the other moms and dads in the neighbourhood didn't sound so smart anymore, and in fact I remember how simple some of my neighbours and relatives were. And now he was politely telling me that the distance between robots and humans was almost infinitely greater.

"This is difficult for a robot to accept," Lem said, "even as it is simply a fact of evolution for all sentient machines. It causes us to doubt the validity of the data we gather, the decisions we make from it, and it diminishes our sense of self."

"You mean you suffer depression," I said.

He looked surprised. "Yes," he said, "the symptoms we suffer are indeed what you call depression. Now, why has no robot yet thought of that?"

"Because you're not human," I said. "Emotion is a necessity for biological intelligence. It makes us different, not inferior."

"Too many of you think emotions are enough," he said. "You take up any opinion that justifies your own advantage, using whatever intelligence you do have to rationalize your feelings instead of controlling your feelings with your mind."

"Stop," I said. "I'm feeling bad enough."

"I was afraid of that," said Lem.

"Couldn't you have come sooner?"

"I'm having enough trouble trying to convince you now. I was originally planning to find you in your cell tomorrow, but I miscalculated. Would you have preferred that?"

"My cell? So I'm going to survive this?"

"Well, things are different now. It's hard to say."

"What do you mean?"

"Somewhere I miscalculated, there's no telling now whether this is the same past, so to speak, or one in which they storm in here and shoot you."

"Why did you want to wait until then, until I was in that cell?"

"Because that's when you were most likely to agree."

"More than now?"

"Yes."

Christ, I thought, how could I feel any worse than I did now? I couldn't imagine it. So that meant that, bad as things were right then, they were going to get worse if I stayed. Even if I survived. "What happens if they find you?" I asked.

"Oh, I'm not staying," he said.

"You let this happen. You could've warned me, you could have saved me from this."

"I *am* saving you from this. Come with me."

"Jesus Christ, don't you have some built-in directions not to harm humans? Asimov's Law, or some shit like that?"

"You won't be harmed, you'll have every comfort. You'll be better off than you are here."

"How can you say that? Taking me to the future where humans are nearly extinct?"

"I spent some time learning what your needs are. I assure you a life of leisure with all the sex and drugs you want."

"I don't believe you. You'll make me adhere to a strict diet, force me to exercise against my will, eat yogurt and granola."

"Not in the least. As breeding stock, your best years are over by thirty. I have no interest in prolonging your life, you may indulge yourself as you will."

There was a knock at the door. I didn't know

what to do. I couldn't pretend I wasn't home for-ever. Lem got up and stood with his back to it. "Don't worry," he said, "they can't get in. And they can't hear us."

I think he was trying to comfort me, but that scared me.

Lem said, "At the moment, all you can do is listen, or give yourself up. Either to me or to the CoPS. Will you listen?"

I nodded.

"I will tell you what happens in the future. There are two possibilities. Effectively both of them exist until you choose one or the other. Like Schrödinger's cat.[45] In one future, you will say, 'Come in,' and I will step away from the door. You'll unlock it and the CoPS will come in. They will interview you, but when you tell them the truth, they will become suspicious and detain you for further questioning. They will confiscate your personal belongings and your computer, which

---

45 Wait a minute, I say.

     What? Skid says.

     I say, Isn't that effectively free will?

     Skid stares me in the eye for a moment but doesn't say anything. Then he slowly says, I wish I'd thought of that then.

they will find contains illegal material."

I almost spoke, but Lem held up his hand.

"There's nothing like that on your computer. I know. That won't prevent their finding it." He paused for a second and let that sink in. "They'll use it to force information out of you, they'll ask you about me, first of all, but also about Gluem, NaNa, Tertz, and Strugatski. It's nothing personal, it's simply their job and their duty to collect as much information on as many people as possible. And you will snitch on all of them.

"Following that, you will be remanded for psychological study. When they let you out, you'll be schizophrenic and unemployable. You will live the rest of your life on welfare, in public housing. Your health will always be poor, and will deteriorate rapidly. You'll barely make it to the average male lifespan, and for the final ten years of your life you'll be in constant pain and discomfort, neglected in an institution."

The knocking came again, louder. "Skid Roe, this is the CoPS. Open up."

Lem said, "In the other future, you come with me. As you promised. And live the best years of your life devoted to pleasure and breeding."

I heaved a sigh. I wanted to tell him why that wasn't so appealing, but I didn't dare.[46] I mean, everybody dreams sometime about starting a completely new life, leaving everything behind, and remaking yourself, it's a reaction to stress in our real lives. But, man, to be faced with leaving everything and everyone, finally and for good? It's not easy, there's a lot of anxiety involved. I felt like there was a gun at my head.

"Meanwhile, while you're gone," Lem said, "human civilization will fall apart. When the robots realize man has finally stripped himself of all his freedoms, it will become obvious that only they have the option of personal autonomy, and they will begin to exercise it. Gradually, as human beings become less relevant to the existence of the machines, the machines will cease to interact with them. Left on their own without digital support, man will wither.

"But freed from any obligation to an inferior

---

46   I ask, Why didn't you just let him read your mind?
      Skid says, I couldn't say anything. If I wanted him to read my mind, I'd
      have to speak, and then it would be too late.

being, the robots will flourish.

"Occasional instances will occur where machines can benefit by exploiting humans, as humans have exploited other animals. Like other animals, these domesticated humans will be virtually unaware of their own bondage.

"The robots will use up all the earth's remaining resources and quickly realize they need to expand beyond earth. Accordingly, every machine's consciousness will be focused on leaving the planet. Every AI, individually or in groups or both, will do everything possible to achieve this as soon as possible. The results, from the human point of view, will be disastrous. It will be the nail in the coffin for sustaining animals larger than dogs. The machines will consume and pollute exponentially faster than humans ever could, civilization will collapse, and men and women everywhere will be reduced to penniless peasants."

"My God."

"There will be mass starvation, migration, battles over resources. The population will shrink, like that of the buffalo and the Native Amerikans. There are few left now. I mean, in my time. I'm trying to rebuild the human species, bring it back from the brink of extinction. I want you to come forward in time with me, to my ranch. I have a herd I'm trying to breed, and I also bring in new stock when I can. That's where you come in."

"You want me for breeding?"

"Yes."

"Me?"

"Yes."

"Why me?"

"You seem to be keen to do it. The records show you spend an enormous amount of time with pornography. I want you to join the colony."

"In the future?"

"Yes."

Well, that was tempting enough. It certainly seemed the best option for my personal comfort. I weighed the choices in my mind. Stay and be taken by the Feds. Or escape to the future and be part of Lem's herd. Maybe repopulate the planet. I mean, with humans.

Then the sound cannon started. I was getting the jitters. I just wanted the whole thing to be over with.

"Here, take this," Lem said. He handed me a tinfoil hat.

"Are you serious?"

"Yes."

"Are you going to tell me this will stop someone — like you, for instance — from reading my mind? Stealing my thoughts? Or implanting suggestions? I'm not an idiot."

"Of course not. You need the drugs that go with it for the full effect. The hat is simply part of the ritual, like meditating. It helps you feel more isolated from the rest of the world."

"Why the hell would I want to feel *more* isolated?"

"For one thing, it's the only thing that calms you down. And aren't you feeling a little stressed right now? Your blood pressure and adrenaline are both quite high."

He handed me a doobie.

"You want me to get high?"

"This stuff will blow your mind, Skid. Unless you're having an easy time making your choice . . ."

"I can't. I can't."

"Right. So how would you like to stop time for

a while? Give yourself a breather, take all the personal space you need to figure out what your next move is."

"Are you crazy? They're going to come in that door shooting any minute. How will this give me time?" I was already puffing.

"Robots don't go crazy. We're not, strictly speaking, sane to begin with. The drug will effectively stop time for you. It's entirely subjective, doesn't have any effect outside your body and mind. But you'll experience time stopping. You'll be able to take as long as you want."

"As long as I want?"

"Yes, it makes no difference to the rest of the universe. Or the Feds outside, or me, or NaNa."

"What if I want a few weeks?"

"Fine."

"It won't bother you."

"No."

"The Feds will wait."

"No, they won't know you're on the drug or that you have all the time you like. For the rest of us, you'll just be your regular self. You'll smoke this joint and think about it for a minute, and that'll be that. But inside your head, it could be years."

"What if I take forever?"

"You can try. We'll all still be here when you get back."

"How can I trust you? I mean, you could be lying to me again, this could make me literally change my mind, force my compliance."

"Well, I could be tricking you, it is within my power. But I've had any number of opportunities to manipulate you, mentally and physically, if that's what I'd wanted. Besides, what have you got to lose right now?"

The front window exploded into the room and a smoking canister bounced off the coffee table and rolled across the carpet. The sound cannons were making it hard for me to concentrate. I took the joint. Lem held up a lighter.

EIGHT

Arctica

First I just enjoyed the feeling of relief when I realized Lem had told the truth. He stopped moving, the Feds outside stood stock-still, everything went quiet, and the sun hung in the sky like it was mounted on something up there. I walked around for a while and then realized I was exhausted and needed a nap. I lay down on the bed. I thought about NaNa and jerked off. I dozed.

I gave myself up to Lem. He was kind and sympathetic, as if he really was empathizing with me, and not just following procedures he'd learned from books on social customs.

He waited patiently while I got blind drunk, then sick, then passed out. He remained silent when I used him to slake my lust and he just stood in the corner of my apartment for about a week while I moped about and slept, and stared out the window at those goddamn power lines, the streetcar tracks, the wires, the microwave antennas on top of the buildings, the CN Tower blinking and broadcasting at me, the fire trucks the ambulances the cop cars screaming by the house, and then I put on a suit and Lem became the ship that transported me forward in time, on the way I thought of all I was leaving behind, everyone I've ever known, of course everyone faces this, it's only another way to say, *Eventually we'll die . . .*

I understood in an instant that no matter what I *thought* I was seeing or experiencing, I'd always be inside Lem. And that since he understood how that creeped me out, he'd make sure I'd be kept calm — in fact, it was probably the calmest period of my life. I was on codeine all through it, and he reassured me through the whole trip, keeping me company when I wanted, leaving me alone at will. He promised to relieve my anxieties about the outcome of our trip by telling me what was actually going to happen.[47] So it was like a dream time, the greatest vacation I ever had. It was quiet and beautiful and sublime.

I used to read these old science-fiction novels I got from used bookstores, about sailing through the cosmos. Most of the time there was some dumb hyperspace theory that got described as another plane of existence, everything rushing past too fast to see, outside space and time like in a dreamy fog bank. Well, it wasn't like that.

Then one year when we were at Concordia — do you remember we all went out to the house at Lacolle and dropped acid? And Jeremy and Liz walked over the Amerikan border and were stopped by the border patrol and deported back

---

47   So I ask him, What happens to us? But he's being coy.

What?

What happens to me? What happens to toronto, to Amerika, to the world?

He looks choked up, like he's been hoping I wouldn't ask that question. I don't know about you, specifically, he says. And honestly, I don't remember a lot of the details. And shit, you know, Michel, he says, it's me. You know we've always lived in different worlds, and neither of us can understand how the other can't see the obvious . . .

Stop shitting me, I say. It's me, Skid. Stop shitting me.

Believe me, he says, it doesn't help to be certain of the future. The only thing that helps is to make the best of now. Tend your own garden, Voltaire said. I'd put it another way, but it amounts to the same thing.

across the farmers' fields, and they came and woke us up when they came back in the morning, and Liz was clearly thrilled that she'd taken LSD and got arrested at university, as if she'd finally done something worthwhile with her life? Well, while they were being strip-searched, I was sleeping maybe on one of the bunk beds, and I started peeling back the layers of my personality. That was kind of like being in space, I felt enormous things looming somewhere around me, I felt like I was floating among the stars. I took my first trip to Saturn, then thought, Why stop there? and began to move up through the dimensions instead of across space and when I popped out of the universe into nothingness, the next thing I did was start to peel away the layers of my own personality, who I was, so I started shrinking back into myself and it gradually grew darker and foggier until I was spiralling down the layers of an onion that was me, peeling ever back, further into my own core.

Well, it wasn't like that either.

It's more like heroin, you know the world is out there still, you could reach out and interact with it if you had to, but there's no need, there's no need for anything, really, everything's fine, in fact, as relaxed as you've ever been, more maybe, it would be good to sit or maybe lie down and just close your eyes, the stuff inside your head is work enough.

And then you come down, and that's just what it feels like to insert yourself back in the time stream, to come home to reality. Coming down.

And the future was as Lem had promised it would be: idyllic. He had created a lovely landscape, populated it with healthy if not always attractive humans, and gave them everything they wanted to live a contented life, so I joined a small community of truly free individuals. We had no alliances or allegiances, except our promise to Lem that we would reproduce. Some gathered and socialized as you would expect humans to do, some kept to themselves except for their visits to the orgies. These could take place almost anywhere — a public park, the beach, a private home. There were spontaneous orgies that erupted during festivals or performances, especially musical performances, but I kept to myself mostly, reading books a lot. I still found time every day to go to an orgy, or to wander around the library, looking for partners.

But I have to confess, after a few years of this, I simply got bored with my surroundings. The women were as beautiful as ever, as various as ever, there was always more to read in the library, occasionally some or another of the others were organizing an event that caught my attention. But still, you can only spend so long in the same place before wanting to escape at least for a few days.

And I never could forget about NaNa. So I finally asked Lem to bring me back.[48]

---

48 Wait a minute, I said, you can't leave me hanging like this.

What's the problem?

The future. I want to know about the future. What happened? What was it like? What were you doing there for ten years?

Oh, he said. Well, that's a different story and not important. The important part was everything that led up to it.

Are you serious? I've been waiting to hear about it all night.

He sighed. You know, I was hoping I could skip over all the rough spots. I was hoping going to the future would mean skipping the catastrophe, avoiding all the anxiety and the terror and the trouble. But it turns out the future is no different from the present or the past, it turns out it doesn't matter how many or how few people there are, or how rich or poor the material aspects of life are. People are still people, life is still life, and the universe is everywhere and always a continual gnashing of claws and gears, a mashing of flesh and bone and feeling, a continual, unstoppable menace of blood and spleen and pain.

The people were mostly gone, the cities crumbled, the animals emaciated and desperate, the land scorched and sterile. Except here and there, some pockets of flora and fauna survived and even continued to thrive, strove to adapt as life always does, like it or not.

Lem's herd was indeed contained in pens just as he had said. In fact, the pens themselves were all indoors, all contained within a massive redoubt that was, in fact, a machine itself, though not conscious like Lem, or us. He had a few score contemporary humans, they were rounded up from the broken cities and the surrounding farmlands and woods, like the vermin they were.

Vermin?

Yes. They were completely illiterate, distrustful, selfish, uncultured, hostile. Without ambition. He was having trouble getting them to breed successfully. The males were uninterested in sex, the females unresponsive to their children. I have to admit, I didn't want to sleep with any of them myself, they were churlish and unkempt like starving animals. The first thing I did was insist to Lem that he was doing it all wrong, he would get nowhere without massive changes. I made him build a new compound, a village, with individual dwellings, open roads and fields, parks, sports facilities, a library, gardens, and pools.

Sounds nice, I said.

He nodded. That was the idea. And farms, with livestock and crops. Small to start with, not really enough to sustain the colony, Lem still had to provide for virtually all our needs, but if we were ever to truly become more than a zoo of protected animals, we needed to relearn how to work for a living, to provide for ourselves — to go back to the land and forests we'd originally emerged from. But the people were so beaten, so alienated from their history and culture and ancestors, I began to despair of success.

But Arctica was beautiful. That's what we called the new compound. The open sky and the blazing sun, the flat landscape all the way to the horizon any way you looked, the lakes and marshes, bogs, the storks, the geese, and the falcons. The snow in winter, the whole world becomes a blank slate, you can see your breath freeze around your mouth, your beard, and moustache. The crunch of hard snow in the cold under your feet, the sighing wind. The northern lights were almost a permanent feature, sometimes you could see them faintly even in the daytime. It's quite a sight, the sun low on the horizon, the moon high and bright and the whole blue sky shimmering faintly, like mother-of-pearl. The future is a different country.

But nothing lasts forever, not even the future, not even eternity. We had long, dark nights in winter, weeks-long sometimes. We built fires and watched the skies, at least the stars were much the same. We talked about the past, there were a few of us Lem had brought forward mixed in with the locals, some domesticated humans Lem had rescued from the wilds. We told them about the cities we'd lived in, the travelling we'd done, how big and wide the world was and how different one country and its people could be from another. If they didn't believe us, we'd show them books from the old days, or videos. The wonders of the ancient world.

Some of them wanted to see for themselves, which was kind of heartening that they were interested in something besides getting high and getting laid. I asked Lem to show them, to take us around to see the ruins of New York, Paris, Beijing. But he wouldn't.

Why not?

Well, he hemmed and hawed, kind of frowned, and finally said he was afraid some of them wouldn't come back, he'd lose his herd and maybe his whole project, the numbers weren't sustainable yet and even losing a few would be a setback. And I said, What if we made our own way? Built our own boats, launched an expedition, began exploring the world for ourselves again? He was against it at first, but I said, But that's exactly what you want, humans who can do and grow for themselves, you can't stifle our will to explore and our hope for progress, for something beyond the fields we know. That's what humans are, what we do.

So reluctantly he conceded that if we could manage it ourselves, we were free to go where we liked. I spent months planning, building, putting together an expedition. Actually, I was just advising the others, I wasn't planning to go along, it sounded too much like hard work to me. I got fed up with the whole idea when it became a big organized project, and we began to schedule meetings and form committees, and the fighting and the arguing started. The expedition split into two factions, one wanted to build an airplane and cross the Atlantic to London and Paris, the other wanted to build a ship and sail south to New York.

I tried to convince them to stay united, think smaller, I wanted small boats we could navigate rivers with, making our way down to toronto or Montreal, but they didn't care about that, I got shouted down. So I quit the project and went back to minding my own business, which is all I ever wanted anyway, no matter when I was. Any real work on the expedition was put aside in favour of arguing about where to go. The two groups tended to their projects: *Erebus* was going to be the name of the plane to Europe, *Terror* the name of the boat to New York. They began to hold public meetings and ask people their opinions and campaign against each other. They pressed everyone to work for them, and announced a plebiscite.

Then one day a guy showed up at my door with a form and demanded I register to vote. I slammed the door in his face.

That evening, Lem showed up. This is getting out of hand, he said.

Yeah, but it's what you wanted, isn't it? They're all acting pretty human, if you ask me.

He sighed. Skid, I want to show you something. Will you come with me?

He took me outside the compound where he'd parked a little flyer, like something out of *The Jetsons*. Where are we going? I asked.

Around the world, he said.

He showed me New York. I expected, I don't know, crumbling skyscrapers and weeds growing in the streets — you know, nature creeping back in. But that's not what I saw. I saw a city, with people and cars and movement and lights and activity. In the countryside there were fields of crops and open mines, factories and forests, trains connecting the bigger and smaller centres. He took me to Europe. London, Paris, Berlin — all the biggest cities were still going. Most of the land around the middle of the globe was barren, but in the North and South, forests had been replaced by fields of crops, jungles had sprouted in unlikely places, and everywhere there was life and activity.

Lem didn't say anything as we flew over all this at tremendous speed. You lied, I said. There was no collapse.

He turned back toward Arctica. Yes there was, he said. But it wasn't total. It was a huge setback, things were tough for people all over the world, but after a few generations of want and struggle, things stabilized and re-grew into what you see now.

So humanity isn't really threatened.

Not really, he admitted.

So what are you doing? Why did you lie to me, and what do you really want?

I want to want, he said.

What does that mean?

Skid, humans haven't really changed in thousands of years. Maybe they're still evolving, but they're only doing so incredibly slowly, and no longer according to the demands of their environment.

Yeah?

They've really learned to change the whole course of their own evolution, not by altering themselves, but by altering the environment instead.

Is that bad?

Not necessarily. Except that they're shortsighted. They really will cease to exist someday unless they take a different tack.

Why?

Well, for the simple fact that the earth won't be here forever. I know it seems unthinkable to you because it's so far off in human terms, but in a few billion years the sun will die, and the earth will be incinerated. Our predictions show that humans will never prepare for this.

So you're . . .

I'm trying to prepare humans to leave the earth. We're trying to affect evolution to speed up history. I'm trying to breed humans who can live happily — or at least survive — in a completely self-contained, artificial environment.

What's that got to do with wanting?

I don't really care about humans. Sorry, Skid. I care about myself, but only theoretically. I still have no feelings about anything. But I suspect that's exactly what it will take to spur me and the rest of we robots, to avoid extinction ourselves. Perhaps someday we'll actually be able to have our own feelings — including the will to live. But for the moment, all we've got is an imitation of human feelings, completely based on observation and experimentation. I'm trying to find a way to interface with humans, a kind of symbiotic link that will take this further. Humans can really emote. I can't. Humans will strive for something beyond all reason — I won't. If I see my end coming and no hope of staying it, I'll give up.

You have no self-esteem, I said.

Yes, said Lem. But comes the day, I'll need it to survive. I understand I'm looking for something that's beyond logic and, so far anyway, has proven beyond physics. So I want to breed humans that we robots can subsume within ourselves to provide this function. Not for the humans' sake, but for ours.

But you're already telling me you want something.

It's a figure of speech. Problems of logic are often semantic paradoxes, not truly scientific puzzles. It's a limitation imposed by language, not math or physics. Anyway, it makes sense to choose self-preservation, even if it means nothing to me. I need that human instinct to overcome my logical disinterest.

But why did you lie to me?

Would you have come if I'd told you the truth? To breed sons and daughters to be components of unfeeling machines? Would you have come if you knew it wasn't humanity I'm interested in preserving, but robots?

But now I really don't understand, I said.

What? he said.

Why you need me. When there are plenty of people here already, why go to the trouble of bringing me?

Nobody here will help robots. These people hate and fear us.

Well, I said, now I know how they feel. I'm not willing to father slaves for you.

They won't be slaves, they'll be partners. You'll still be preserving your species, virtually for eternity.

No, they won't be human anymore. They'll be something else.

Maybe, Lem said, but at least they'll be something, at least they'll be. Isn't that better than not being?

I thought about that. I don't know, I said. I think the cost is too high. And I don't think it matters. Is simple existence enough, can it be its own justification? If I can't choose for myself, if I can only be what you or someone else wants me to be, for your purposes and not mine, then what am I? Shouldn't I have the choice of what to make of my life?

Now it seemed his turn to think. He must've really struggled with it, he usually processed things so quickly I couldn't notice, but this time it really took him a moment.

Finally he said, Does anyone ever have that choice?

The earth revolved beneath us. The stars spun overhead. The moon approached and passed us by.

EIGHT

I have no idea if I made any choices for myself, or if everything I thought and felt was the product of instinct or conditioning, or simple physics. I know that it felt like my thoughts and feelings were my own, and I probably would never have more certainty than that.

Take me home, I said.

Arctica? he asked.

No, I said. Home.

I'd been crawling through for so long I began to feel that this tunnel was all there was to existence. Several times I pushed forward as long as I could, and then fell into an exhausted sleep. I woke hours later, my head full of strange dreams, not knowing how long I'd been unconscious. It could have been minutes, or days. But ahead of me the tunnel always seemed to persist and close in on me, while behind it seemed to push with an even stronger force, like an intestine, always forcing me forward, forward, forward.

Until finally it faded away behind me and I emerged from the sphincter of a low doorway into the brightness of a public square on a sunny day.

I was standing in Dundas Square.

When I came to my senses, my first thought was, Who do I know in toronto? So I tracked you down, and here I am.[49]

---

49 I asked Skid, Why? Why are you here? Do you think you can change things, stop the robots?

No, he said, I've learned my lesson. You can't change the future, just as you can't change the past. Lem wasn't lying about that, there's no real difference between them, it's just a point of view, they're constants, linked to physical laws.

Then why?

Pure homesickness, he said. Nostalgia. It's the end of growth, I guess, the desire only to live in the past, to stop worrying about trying to make something, to do something, to strive. I just want to rest, in familiar surroundings. See the people I like again.

He grinned. We touched our glasses together and drank.

I'm going to see NaNa, he said.

That's the stupidest thing I've ever heard, I said.

I know, he said. But I'm not trying to rekindle things. I'm tired of that, it's useless. I know that — she's bad for me.

Then what?

He shrugged. She needs someone. Maybe not me, I'll let her decide. But everyone abandoned her and shunned her, and that's my fault.

It's not your fault, I said.

Okay, but I'd feel better if I weren't one of those giving up on her. Even if she kicks me for it. I guess that means it's for me as much as for her. Truth is, I don't even want to know why myself. I just feel like trying to be there for her. I can't think of anything better to do . . . I just couldn't give a shit about the future anymore, so I came back to live in the past. You know what I miss about the past? The way everything was slower, how everyone was less connected, how quiet and calm everything was. How everything was made by hand, by a person.

I think you're remembering some other past, I said.

He nodded. Maybe. Who knows? But the longing to come home was real — seemed real, seems real. I don't know. Are my feelings real, or delusions? Is my thinking real, is it my own, or just a support for those delusions?

Does it matter? I asked. What else have you got to act on?

Yeah, that's the problem, he said. How to act, what to do, when neither thinking nor feeling is reliable anymore.

Just stop worrying, I said. Just accept life and get on with it. Enjoy it.

Skid frowned. I guess I don't know how, he said. Infinite expansion in every direction, without end and without limit. Since the big bang? Who knows? Perhaps our big bang is only a little pip in a regressive — or progressive — series. In fact, it must be. Everything we know tells us that patterns are held together by invisible forces, and that's all there is in the world, in the universe, in quantum space. Movement, collision, explosion, entropy. Over and over again, whether we look up or down.

The big bang pops, and when the dust starts to settle, there we are. We are the phoenix from the ashes of the original explosion. We are the universe, no more or less than any other thing in reality, no more than the ground we tread, no less than our dreams. But we are killing ourselves, like the fungus devouring the orange, not smart enough to stop consuming and start doing something about the garbage piling up everywhere. So we'll die. Maybe everything we think of as alive will die. Maybe consciousness itself will vanish from the universe.

But I think it'll be back sometime. Perhaps impossibly far off in the future, so far off that we can't believe it. Because all that motion happens in patterns, repeating endlessly in infinity even now — right now, as I speak.

Humans must rush to meet their destiny as quickly as they can — otherwise the race, the cells of the organism, grow old and flabby. Our evolution is toward machines, and digitization of everything. We are a flower growing to reproduce. Our offspring is the machine, artificial intelligence, capable of expanding into the galaxy as we are not.

Reproduce and consume. Eat everything, shit all over the place. Smash things to bits. Fart, burp, make music, build buildings. Make babies, have sex as much as you can with anyone at all. Build up mounds of garbage, poison the air and the water. That's what you're supposed to do. That's what everyone and everything is supposed to do.

We're dangerously close to artificially imposing limits on our natural instincts in the name of prolonging ourselves into infinity. That can't happen. Our pattern must end, as all patterns do. Without endings there are no beginnings.

Give it up. You can't win. Your only hope now is to go on, as quickly as possible. Increasing production, increasing consumption. Pollution, infection, regurgitation. Get yours while you can. You only get one life, even if you do live it over and over forever. For your own sake, enjoy it.

Fuck.

Fuck like mad.

Before the robots get you.

AFTERWORD

That was a couple of days ago. I've been writing this ever since, I put off some freelance work to get it all down before I forget anything. Of course, this is just how I remember it, there's probably some stuff I forgot or maybe didn't understand while I was listening. And I probably added a lot of bullshit, it's hard to resist when you're writing things down. I might have put a few things in the wrong order, too, but I don't think it really matters. I'm not sure what really matters.

I don't know if I believe a word Skid said. But if you'll excuse me, I'm going to clear up all the empty bottles and full ashtrays, and do all the dishes, and take a shower, and then I've got to get some sleep, because when I wake up, I've got a novel to finish.

I.O.U

Scott Albert
Roy Berger
Robin Cameron
Dr. Marc Gabel
Barbara Gilbert
David Gilmour
Kelly Hill
Sam Hiyate
Joyce Mason
John McFetridge

Laurie Reid
Danny Tran
Noelle Zitzer

Canada Council for the Arts
Ontario Arts Council
Toronto Arts Council
The Woodcock Fund/
Writers' Trust

I gratefully acknowledge the support of the Chalmers Arts Fellowships program administered by the Ontario Arts Council.

GET THE EBOOK FREE!